A COUPLE
OF THINGS

BEFORE
THE
END

A COUPLE OF THINGS BEFORE THE END

STORIES
SEAN O'BEIRNE

To Sall

Published by Black Inc.,
an imprint of Schwartz Books Pty Ltd
Level 1, 221 Drummond Street
Carlton VIC 3053, Australia
enquiries@blackincbooks.com
www.blackincbooks.com

9781760641283 (paperback)
9781743821282 (ebook)

 A catalogue record for this
book is available from the
National Library of Australia

Cover design by Peter Long
Cover image © Trent Parke / Magnum Photos
Text design and typesetting by Marilyn de Castro

CONTENTS

SCOUT

Yeah I'm happy to talk about it. I think it's good you're trying to find blokes that were in it. What did I learn? What did I *learn*. Lemme think. Probably nothing. Nah, I'm only kidding. Quite a few knots, that's for sure. Nah, to be fair, I think just – being outside. I take my own kids camping now and I don't think I'd do that unless I'd had that experience in the Scouts. We didn't camp as a family, my mum wouldn't go it, she's not gonna stay in some tent. Sometimes we'd go to a caravan park, but Dad, I don't know what he wanted, probly to stay at home. But on weekends now, when I have the kids, we go up to Turra, or the Creskie National Park, we camp there. So, yeah. If it wasn't for Scouts, I never would have got to swim in a freshwater creek, fry stuff up at night, roast potatoes in the fire. And shoot a lot a stuff. Yeah. We did shoot a lot of guns, which was unusual, even in those days, for a troop to go out shooting as much as we did. If we saw other troops, at something like the Queen's

Challenge or something, they never did anything with guns. But I think our troop was a bit more shooty, or there was a little bit of a gun culture there because our leader Sarge was a cop and Knotty the other leader he was a cop too. Lookin back, you wouldn't let any of it happen now. On camp they used to just give us a couple a .22s and let us go for a walk. Me and this other kid Dean McLennan, we used to shoot birds, or one time up on some farm we shot these ceramic things, these weird sort of ceramic bulb things that were left up the top of a lot of these sort of old electricity poles. We were friggin lucky we didn't shoot each other. Who gives a couple of fourteen-year-olds guns and says, 'Boys, go for a walk'? I don't know, it was the seventies, it was a different time. I do give them credit though. Like, at least we were *there*. Knotty had *six* kids, for fuck sake. I went to his house once, to help pick up some stuff I think, and he's got all this Scout stuff, camping gear, and there's kids everywhere and he had this big aviary out the back, all this netting, and he kept chooks loose in the backyard – the whole joint was just full of kids, chooks, tents, crap, more chooks, fuckin I don't know. People did whatever they wanted back then. People were poorer but they had more stuff in a weird way. Knotty's joint was huge. Dusty, but huge. I reckon he was quite mad, Knotty, the big mad bastard, he had all that goin, so many kids already, and he's a cop, which would be a pretty full stressful day sometimes, and he's doin all this extra stuff, takin a bunch a kids camping who are not even his. And Sarge too, Sarge was in the CID, I remember my mother being very impressed with that, he was a detective, but there he was, teaching a pack a dingaling kids how to build a fire. He was no fuckin fool too, we were scared a Sarge. He had this thing on camp where he would get very shitty if a kid had his hands in his pockets. Drove him nuts. Like, when we had jobs to do, putting up the tents, but some kid would be just thinkin about havin a Mars bar, you know, standin there with his hands in his pockets. And Sarge'd fuckin *bellow* at ya, you'd shit yourself, dreamy little idiot, and suddenly fuckin Sarge is there goin, WHAT ARE YOU DOIN STANDIN ROUND WITH YOUR HANDS IN YOUR POCKETS? He'd go apeshit, he'd really open it right out, I DO NOT WANT TO SEE ONE BOY STANDING AROUND THIS CAMP WITH HIS HANDS IN HIS POCKETS. And you'd fuckin pick up anything, pick up the same peg you just put down, pick up a *leaf*, just to make it look like you were doin somethin. Fuckin hell. You could imagine him yellin at his wife cause he found her in the fuckin kitchen with her hands in her fuckin pockets. Still. He did let us have shotguns. We shot shotguns, not just .22s. And a shotgun, that's a big deal for a kid, that's a big gun, they hurt your shoulder. And .303s, we shot .303s. They had a big cartridge – no, a shell, like a big brass shell. I still have some of them somewhere. And I've still got my little Scout shirt somewhere, Jesus. Little badges on it.

Yeah, so the *badges*. I'm tryna remember, the badges were a big deal, that was most of it, like when we weren't camping, you learnt to do these things, tie a knot, and you got the badges. We did the reef knot, the bowline. I could do the bowline. And we went to this thing called the Queen's Challenge, which was a day out in some field somewhere, and you had to do things like build, no, tie, or lash all these poles together, like wooden poles, in a triangle, and make a thing, a, not a boat, fuck, I can't even describe it – we made a *pyramid*. Out of wood. You lashed the poles together, doin all your knots, and you made a sorta three-dimensional triangle. And it was for survival. You made two of them, and you, like, the patrol, you all got up on one and then you positioned the other one in front, and then you all climbed over to the other one, onto that. And it was for survival. Now if you want to ask me in what emergency circumstance would you immediately build two large wooden pyramids, I don't know. I think we were crossing a river? Or snakes. Snake infestation, you gotta get up higher, you need a pyramid. Though I spose the snakes'd get up there too, pretty fast, they'd be all over it, they'd love a wooden pyramid.

Be like a fuckin play centre for those boys. So maybe just the river. Get across the river. It is strange to think it was like that stuff they make people do now on TV, like on those shows where people have to do stuff on an island. *Survivor*. This was a bit like *Survivor* except there were no celebrities and nobody won anything. We just did it, and then we had lunch.

But most of it, I should say, most of it wasn't the camps or something like the Challenge, most of it was just going to the hall on a Tuesday night. And you'd do the badges there. Or do activities, do stuff about wildlife, nature. I remember the hall, the Scout Hall, it was on Ealey Road, there was a big oval, and on the side there was a brown brick hall and that was the Scout Hall. It was just a wooden floor inside and a flagpole. And every Tuesday you'd get your uniform on, your hat, your woggle, all that, and Mum or Dad would drive me there. Funny to think of me in the front seat with all that on, me little scarf, me little hat, though the hat was quite big, had sort of a quite wide brim, like a little mini sombrero. All khaki, though, you're in khaki. I'm twelve when I started, that's when you start, twelve. But the Tuesday, the Tuesday started in front of the flagpole, and your patrol, which is six of you, all the patrols, you all line up in front of the flag and you put your stuff out for inspection. You had to put stuff on the floor. I can't remember what it was, but it was all stuff a prepared boy would have. Because the Scout motto is 'Be Prepared'. So, fuck knows, I don't know. You had to have twenty cents for a phone call, that I remember. You put your twenty cents on the floor. To show you had it. And then after inspection there was a sort of a ceremony to do with the flag, you pulled a bit of rope and then the flag unfolded, unfurled, yeah, and you saluted. Cause there was a particular way you folded the flag up, the order, so it looked like a tiny neat little square, and you'd tuck the rope into that, so then if you gave the rope one tug, the flag would sorta jump right out and *be* there. And then you'd all salute. We'd all salute.

It all sounds a bit bizarre now. Very military. I forgot about the flag. I suppose the guns were a bit military too, but not really in the way we used them. What else? Badges. Knots and badges I think we've covered. Wooden pyramids. I feel I should stress the incompetence of us as a troop. The leaders were good but us boys we were idiots. I remember us goin into this thing, like a check-point, on this hike where you had to do orienteering, have a compass, and pass through all these locations. And we get to the last one, the last location, and there's these two old guys, old Scout leaders, packin up. Loadin their car. And they're like: 'Who are you?' And we're like: 'Eighth Bundoora! Here to report!' And they go: 'It's *over*.

It finished *an hour ago*. Where have you *been*? Why are you still doing something when everyone else is done?' But it wasn't our fault! We got lost in this aqueduct thing. We thought it was a shortcut. It was all through the bush, this sort of concrete open tunnel thing. And we thought, Sweet! We wandered down that for about forty minutes eating fuckin Cheezels, but then it actually led us back into town. All these kids with their little backpacks on and compasses suddenly coming out of the bush and into the main road of Castlemaine and going, 'Oh.' So. Yep. I don't think Sarge ever found out about that one. I think the guy ticked us off so we officially finished. And then we just went really quickly to the carpark. Yep. Eighth Bundoora.

And then I did see that bit where you go on to what's after Scouts, like at fifteen you have to leave Scouts and if you want to go on, you go on to Venturers. Venturers is I think maybe fifteen to eighteen. But I do remember going up that night to Venturers, you just go up to have a look, it's like a information night, and just thinking, Nup. There was one big gooney bloke, big tall gangly red-headed bloke, with his woggle on, eighteen years old, still in the Scouting movement, with his twenty cents on the ground, and even me, a dopey kid, I could tell that something had gone wrong. Venturers just felt like a room full of – something had gone wrong. Like already even in Scouts, by the time you were in high school, you didn't exactly tell everyone what you were doin on a Tuesday night. And then three more years of that, with the gooney bloke. So that night I thought: Nup. That's it. Thank you. And Dad said to me do you want to do karate.

But listen. I don't know who else you're gonna talk to but, if you do find Knotty and Sarge, please do say hello from me? Sarge is probably in a nursing home by now. But if you do find them, say hello, if you see them both, do sort of say thank you, from me. Tell Sarge, tell Sarge to keep his hands out of his pockets.

ROYALS

THE ROYAL YEAR: A REVIEW

This is our review Of The Year we are honest and welcome HONEST critics.

DEC' 2015

United Australians For Constitutional Monarchy

PO Box 4

Chesil, Queensland, Australia, 4920

Thank you again to supporters who enjoy the newsletters, this is the last for the year.

OTHER Royal Groups Say We are Too Much.

But there is a CRISIS Coming and we must Speak Out.

"maxima fidei loquitur"

"Loyalty Speaks The Loudest"

The Queen

No problems. The head of our country continues to give great value. You've got to hand it to her for complete consistency. 50+ years of her Reign & she's still there. And She loves Australia, she has been here many times.

Philip

Some problems but containable. The Media commentary gave out the cry when PM Abbott said we're going to have Australian Knights and the first one is Prince Philip. And it's true some People said the criticisms to us, e.g: He's too old, he's not the Queen why are we giving it to him, it's just confusing Sir Prince Philip what is that? And every time the News Media commentary brought up things he Philip has said, about Native People, Disabled People, Asian people, African people, and More that does create problems. Best is to keep the emphasis on: HE is not the Queen. And emphasis on Knights we like, Sir John Monash he was a Sir as was the female version Dame Nellie Melba.

Charles.

Discussed below.

<u>Camilla.</u>
Discussed below.

<u>Diana.</u>
Very beautiful but unfortunately "nuts." Not a problem
now of course.

<u>William and Kate.</u>
Beautiful couple. It would obviously be better if he didn't
look so very bald. This we can acknowledge "in house."
Outside the emphasis to be on Kate. She obviously very
Healthy. Very Fit. And Good Posture.

<u>Prince Harry.</u>
It's good he has stopped dressing up as a Nazi.

<u>George.</u>
Very good royal baby. Healthy.

<u>Charlotte the new baby.</u>
No problems.

<u>Threats</u>

<u>Looking to The Road Ahead: When Charles becomes</u>
<u>KING</u>

"Causa est non perdidi"

"No Cause is Lost"

We are meeting constantly throughout the year and We
know people will show an enthusiasm gap here and we
need YOUR ideas.

<u>Situation</u>: Recent Surveys and predictions are not good
as members will know Graeme (Lib) has seen private
polling and Lorraine (Tas. Lib.) also did volunteer work
at Lib headquarters on plebiscite matters ("gay" marriage) and did polling on other Questions and she has
confirmed figures post ERII are "the pits".

We appeal to all members and interested parties to
PLEASE help us as time is TICKING AWAY.

The numbers are in, and a Queen gone world is a "difficult" one for us, Charles is THE threat now (Nature
/"Medicine" /Natural Therapies /Lots About Architec-
ture /Personal "look" wrong+There's Camilla) and we
must "get through" as best we can.

It will be a short reign but we must minimise the dam-
age. Clearing ground for William and <u>emphasis</u> on Kate,

and George (ie: the next Generation with More Royal Babies to come. George will produce at 25 or in late 20s worse case scenario (2040).

Members! Fight! for your Kings of the <u>Future</u>.

<u>MERRY XMAS</u> *** <u>MERRY XMAS</u> *** <u>MERRY XMAS</u> ***

HOMAGE TO BARRY HUMPHRIES

Tuesday, 15th July, 1958

<u>Departure Day</u>

Long morning worrying about my cabin trunk. <u>Found</u> my gloves. Mother awful on dock. Mother <u>at</u> me. Asking me <u>three times</u> if I'd written to Murray. I did not write to Murray! I did not write to Murray! I have not SEEN Murray for SIX MONTHS mother. Dear O my Mother I will not marry Murray Faulkner and O my Mother that means I will now be condemned to be all my life a sales girl at <u>Foys</u>. Well, I am going to London. Dad said really nothing all day but gave me £10. Poor Dad.

On board at 8pm. Mother and Dad, Uncle Donald and June, the McGraths, Andersons and my lovely Bib. Uncle Donald gave me a fountain pen. Bib went down with Daddy to throw streamers. All off ship at 10:30. I couldn't see Bibby, she was too small. Last thing I saw was Uncle

Donald pointing and pointing at me or the air I didn't know <u>what</u>, then I thought Oh it's the pen, he's saying use the pen. I did the pen back to him and he did it to me and then thank goodness there was the horn and we started going.

Wednesday, July 16th

Sad about my Bib. Told myself buck up. Ship is nice. Cabin 116/117 'E' deck. Sharing with two girls, one Marion, snores. Other girl Eloise very pretty, going to England to marry English boy who she met at Imperial Wool. Broke strap on my sandal already <u>first day</u>. There is a shop here so let's see. Wore the black courts, not too bad. But you can get bags, shoes, manicures everything on board Eloise says. Then the sensation was - I saw passenger list 1st Class, I knew nobody of course, but in Tourist I saw Mr and Mrs B. Humphries and thought it can't be Barry, but it <u>was</u>. In Main hall, I saw a v thin man going into the public rooms, with hair down to his shoulders. I knew who that was! I went up and he surprised. I think nervous? But nice. I think I was too gay with him and did the <u>talking</u> that mother hates so, had mother's voice in my head of course but I really thrilled to see him its just so wonderful another theatre person is here. I said about the Tivoli 'Arms and the Man' being <u>so</u> awful and he agreed. And the whole company being so much worse since Reg took over. And 'Mr D'Artagnan' even more stinking and those <u>songs</u>. So its beaut we're talking away and then comes his <u>second</u> wife!!!! Rosalind, v tall, New Zealand. Where is Brenda I don't know. I v surprised New Zealand bc Barry was always so <u>mean</u> about New Zealand people, and lo he says he sorry but Rosalind can only speak 'New Zealand dialect'!! He is <u>mad</u>. What a thing to say about your wife. She laughed so maybe its alright.

Thursday, July 17th

Breakfast - porridge. You can have eggs or toast or anchovy toast.
Dinner - cold meat and salad. Jam roly poly.

Pretty breezy on deck.
Supper - grilled fish with chipped potatoes.
Cards Eloise.

Saturday, July 19th

Breezy but a little less.

Went to the Sports deck didn't stay.
Cards Eloise.

Sunday, July 20th

Bored already. The ocean.

Tuesday, July 22nd

Tea with Eloise and Mr and Mrs Phillip Heygate.

Wednesday, July 23rd

Breakfast - porridge.
Went to try find Barry. Should explain to dear Diary. As important perhaps for the future. Barry Humphries is an actor and he is an artist from Melbourne whom I know just a little because I was with him as a fellow actor when the Union Theatre Society did its production of 'The Twelfth Night'. And I was Olivia and Barry was Orsino. He is v eccentric and can be bad.
People who warned me about Barry:
Elizabeth Coates
Jenny Hewitt

That girl at Mrs Haupt's recital

But Dear Diary it was Elizabeth who got into his car after rehearsals and went all the way to Camberwell!!! Elizabeth Coates from MLC! Most inconstant Elizabeth Coates.

But Dear Diary I am wandering from something more serious and getting stuck in the part of me that is not serious and needs to learn. The serious point I want to make is Barry Humphries is an artist who is well known in Melbourne and Sydney and he had a show at the Union Art Gallery which had a bath and the bath had books in it but it was full of custard so that it looked like a person had been sick. On the books. This is 'dada'. Barry Humphries is a 'dada' person. He is a real artist but also is a nice person who can stop being an artist occasionally and talk to people. And he has very long hair. Dada is the art movement that started in Europe in Paris and Berlin after the Great War.

Thursday, July 24th

Long talk with Barry about London and theatre. Problems of Australian theatre. Not enough people. I mean audience. So they're commercial. Only revues. No classics, no cabaret. Barry says 40 theatres in just West End and supper clubs galore. Piccadilly and Soho. Greek St the best but are others. Wish I could remember more. Cabaret. Kurt Vial. I don't know this. Very European. He loves all things from Berlin. He knows a lot about music. I said Handel and Schubert but he said Satie. Painters <u>Whistler</u> also <u>Condor</u> (is Australian). Zara in Zurich was the start of the really new time. But even when Picasso first exhibited the critics said he was a madman, literally a madman and people tried to hit the paintings with their canes.

Supper in Tourist class lounge. Cards Eloise.

Friday, July 25th

~~£144~~ £154
Aunt E's 1/2s a week West Hampstead
All R.A.D.A. £30/9s
Hampstead £? all meals tickets
If I train to Edinburgh Aunt W – ticket 2s/1d and dinners
If I don't that's £2 probably

~~To whom it may concern~~
To the manager,
Dear Sir,
Please allow me to introduce myself, my name is

Dear Sir,

I am a young actress ~~wishing to enquire~~ enquiring as to the possibility of an audition

I am writing to enquire about auditions at your school.

To the Registrar,
Royal Academy of Dramatic Art,
Gower St,
London W.C.1

Dear Sir,

~~I am a young actress wishing to enquire enquiring as to the possibility of an audition at~~

I am writing to enquire about auditions at your school and the dates upon which auditions are held. I wrote for information and a prospectus while still in Australia and you very kindly advised me to write to you once I had arrived in England. My address ~~will be~~ is 27 Aldgate Road, West Hampstead, London N.W.3.

I enclose letters from Mr R. Lawler, playwright and director, of the Union Theatre Society at the University of Melbourne, and Mrs U. Haupt, Dramatic and Elocution Teacher, Hawthorn Academy of Dramatic Arts.

Tuesday, July 29th

Hot. Wrote to Andersons.

Friday, August 1st

'Crossing the line' today which is games when you cross
the equator. Sailors dressed up some in grass skirts. I was
rather bashful to see purser in grass skirt he is a v large
person. We had singsong 'Oh, Jasper' and King Neptune
came and threw landlubbers in the pool. Eloise in the
thick of it so I thought I'd better be a pal. Dunked twice.
Water up nose a great deal. Headache. Eloise too tired
for cards. I wrote to mother.

Saturday, August 2nd

Rain. <u>Barry</u> at morning tea. We talked about Schubert,
and the lieder and especially 'Erlkonig'. He smokes too
much. Where <u>is</u> Rosalind? She is the mystery wife. His
hair is v strange, v black and straight. The most enor-
mous eyes. He is like a Spanish person. Not attractive I
think. I forgot to say Dear Diary what Barry Humphries
famously <u>did</u> as Orsino in 12th Night. He did <u>not</u> like the
play so he became really v bad, he was so awful and <u>so</u>

naughty at Echuca hiding Nigel who played Feste's lute and then making Orsino into a hunchback!! People still ask me abt it, I've had to tell oodles of people and it's all true. It was at Echuca Mechanics Hall and he got I think tights and put them up costume on his back and made the biggest 'hump', horrible, then entered for opening scene - 'If music be the food of love, play on'!! I was off-stage left saw Nigel really crimson up-stage he exited & said to Jim he refusing to play the lute or be in any sc. Orsino is, but Jim says we have to get to the end like this. It was a trial every time Cesario said my Lord Orsino is here I frowned and looked above him otherwise I knew it would be giggles. Pamela Craig said Echuca people at interval saying I didn't know there was a humpback in this one!! I think at the time half cast thought it amusing half not. Jim not. Nigel v not. It was a sad finish tho, next day no Barry, we all say where is he?? and found out Nigel telephoned to Ray and Barry ordered back to Melbourne. And we went up all of N.S.W. w Nigel as Orsino. And Nigel was awful. Worse than Barry really.

Monday, August 4th

Arrived Colombo. Off at 8am in small boats then cab. Saw many bungalows. Then sari market. Eloise v determined bought 3 dresses and bangle all for 40 rupees from tiniest little man. Tea - Galle Hotel. Eloise, Marion, Phillip and Frances, Lt. Cullen, and Mr Newton-Smith and his wife I think ~~Catherine~~ Caroline.

Back onboard at 6:30 pretty tired.

Tuesday, August 5th

Nothing much. Played some quoits. Too hot all day.

Wednesday, August 6th

Barry tea on 'B' deck. Rosalind has colic! They gave Barry chalky medicine for her.

Thursday, August 7th

Tea Barry.

Friday, August 8th

Barry. I wore the summer dress.

Saturday, August 9th

Must write Dad. Costume for ball. Must cards Eloise.
Be friendly.

Sunday, August 10th

Ball - ask steward cloth.

Eloise = Guinevere.
Marion = A sultan.
Me = Joan of Arc.   Sword. paint. ?
Me = Ophelia   ?

Monday, August 11th

Barry luncheon. I said about the Debussy 'Pagodes' that
it too sweet and the Toccata and he thought that too.
Rachmaninov.
Delius but very English.
Satie.

Tuesday, August 12th

Barry

Wednesday, August 13th

Waited for Barry on Rec 2 hours.

Wednesday <u>later</u>

Barry nice to me.

Friday August 15th

Barry

Sunday

Even though I know I have been wrong about him and I know it didn't mean anything - I <u>knew</u> what he was but I didn't learn anything I didn't know, I wanted so much to try and talk to him and be his friend but it <u>was</u> more, to me and to him I think, I <u>can't</u> understand him he is the <u>queerest</u> person there is something inside him bad and <u>dead</u> and I think is <u>not fair</u> even though I know it's not his fault, he has been very maltreated by his mother and other people. It is only ever <u>his</u> feelings that matter but those feelings are demons. He <u>said</u> he would come to the ball but he came with <u>Rosalind</u> of course you little fool she is his wife and she is pretty and <u>taller</u> but he is <u>mad</u> they came not in costumes at all but awful old suits he said to people he was <u>Earle Page</u> and she was in a suit just like his he said she was supposed to be <u>Arthur Calwell</u> what is <u>that</u> supposed to be? None of the English people had ever <u>heard</u> of Earle Page or horrible Arthur Calwell. People were in such lovely costumes and he didn't say a word to me I couldn't even go near him or speak to him, there was such an awful feeling everywhere because they weren't in proper costumes and because of his hair and he kept going to the bar or the bar cart not even dancing just going to the bar cart it was just horrible and Phillip said 'I think that man's had enough' and I saw B take a <u>whole bottle</u> of wine from the bar cart and grinning at people in a <u>mad</u> way I said to Phillip <u>please</u> take it away from him and Phillip did and made Barry sit and eat something but then people were just <u>screaming</u> Barry I don't know <u>why</u> how <u>could</u> he be so drunk he got a whole beef wellington from the <u>Captains table</u> and put it on the <u>dance floor</u> and trying to sing a song to it no-one understood and then just yelling in that horrible vulgar voice Earle Page! really bawling it and Phillip and the other men got Barry by the arms and the whole room watching and Rosalind trying to get the pieces of it in napkins off the floor and the sailors and the purser were there and then Barry fell on the floor and he was sick on the floor. It was absolutely horrible. Eloise took me back here and I don't think I've ever cried so much, I don't know why. He's not mine I'm not that stupid. I don't care if he's mad. I think he's better than other people but he has to look after himself and I don't think other people will look after him. I wish I could see him and could talk to him just once.

Monday

I can't go to him because he's in the brig. I'm not his wife.

Tuesday, August 19th

Nothing. The men say they'll get off at Port Said and wait for another ship.

Wednesday, August 20th

I redid my cabin trunk. Bought a hat.
2s/1d.
Cards Eloise.

JACK

MEMOIRS OF A LIFE
BY JOHN VANCE O'CONNELL "JACK"

In these memoirs I begin to recollect a world which was here even though it seems hard to believe as I sit in my unit with TV remote, etc but not that long ago it was shanks pony as the only transport, kerosene for lighting, bath once a week in the copper bowl in the washhouse, chopping wood and other activities now fallen out of favour. When I was a lad in Crenella area c. 1938 we killed our own meat pigs and sheep, offal in a bucket up to Mum, lights to the dogs and the cat got the tongue, young people don't know that when we say cat got your tongue that means the cat really got it. This is another reminiscence my father used to get a tongue from a cow and hang it over the fence with his head behind so it looked like his tongue much to the merriment of us kids.

I am writing these my remembrances for children,

grandchildren, etc., friends of the family at age of 88 years to set down for the record some of how it was in the old days, I find increasingly the young ones don't know any of this and we elderly can be of some use instructing on a world that was hard where everything now is so easy, Mobile phones, etc.

And in memory of my twin brother Terence Francis "Terry" who recently passed away, my brother and friend for 88 years.

My father Daniel Vance O'Connell was seventh child of seven, the only one of his four brothers never to make a good living, he never found his profession but knocked from job to job, his true profession was drinking, playing the clown, the entertainer, etc, telling riddles that was all he was good at, never owned his own home, paid rent all his life. His father Michael Francis O'Connell farmed sheep and cattle at Murra Murra approx. 5 km south west of Clondale, died when son Daniel three years old. Daniel my father the Old Boy we always called him was on "susso" government paid labour in Tentertown and Petong 1930/31, c. 1930s worked in wool sheds outside Lochnea and Mangatta, he was a big man strong enough but no application he couldn't pay attention to anything. The Old Boy he was always the same he would sit and talk for hours, he played the harmonica or banjo when he could get one and had a great love of "jokes" and funny sayings all of which I have forgotten although the end of one still sticks in my mind, he used to tell Terry and I a riddle or I suppose joke, about two other twin boys called Tit and Tat and the joke was when they were infants there was no tit for Tat. He told that many times and played the banjo.

In 1937-38 he went share farmer that's a live in jobbing farmer you don't own anything at "Roscommon" for Dick Henley who also owned the tannery at Catters's Point, then us kids went to stay with Coglan family while the Old Boy was Wool scourer at Breakwater for Eyre & Dunleavy wool merchants, then Powys & Sons in Newall St, Geelong, wheeling wool bales and only got that because Pat Brennan our cousin took pity on him, years later old Pat told me the Old Boy was not much good for anything "Delirium tremens" could only bring in lunch for the others try and tell riddles and jokes to which he was addicted before going off again to the pub. Mum kept him in the back room at Reuben Rd where he had a kerosene tin next to his bed to throw up into. Ended with seizures and strapped to bed in North Geelong hospital, Kiora Rd, myself, Terry and Mum visiting him on several occasions, Nurses unable to say what was wrong with him, "Heart or Stroke or Flu, we Don't Know" strapped down because would attack the nurse or doctors during seizure, etc. Died 2.5.57, aged 55 years.

My mother Lillian Mary Breen b. 1903 always known as 'Lil' did it all and was the rock of us, raising us boys, always sweeping and sewing Mum, helped by many cups of tea, very handy with a needle, made all our clothes including pants, overalls, etc., for Terry and me made out of old calico bags! So we always had enough clothes and Mum was even able to make us blue suits out of serge really for sofas for Terry and me on occasion of our first communion at St Aloysius in Ballarat, Bishop Gorman officiating on the day. Terry in a great state I recall because very concerned we would be up the back of the procession for the blessed sacrament as many poorer boys were because their family could not afford the proper tailor's suit and they were only in homemade suits like us or tired old jumpers. I was more bothered with that hot suit very uncomfortable and itching!

Mum passed away 22.8.87 aged 84 years at Grace McKellar home in Geelong prior to Grace McKellar Mum was at 33 Yule St Belmont, in a unit I built for her on land snapped up as a lot of two zoned residential, bought for 1200 pounds when blocks were selling in Corio same size £3000.

Family was yours truly eldest born 12.4.26 and Terry delivered minutes after me forceps delivery and internal problems never spoken of in those days of course. After us boys Mum could have no more kids, a cause of shame for Mum in country town where others more productive, very judgemental times and staid old attitudes, I suppose people thought you needed a big family to get the work done, though most boys fled the farm as soon as they bloody could of course so it made no difference. This did not stop entire district full of Catholics all dead set mad to get more children. Coglan's next farm had eleven.

Recollections of early life stand out including happier memories of us kids being given sandwiches with plum jam at Coglan's farm only 3 miles away or Mick Coglan would let us boys ride with him on back of hay binder which was used to cut open hay and had six horses to pull it which we found wonderful to see, we would get on and ride or be even allowed to hold the reins.

Also the Gillies farm approx. 7 miles from our farm proud possessors of a "AWA" Radiola wireless set I remember well, a most impressive brown Bakelite object that had us crowding round every Saturday arvo to hear the 3LO match of the day with Reg Soames commentator and sports personality who was later done many will recall for financial mismanagement in Resolute public investment scheme in 1970s under Hamer state government. I was football mad in those days a big supporter of Melbourne then known as the Fuchsia's, I would practice on the tear and bouncing it, kicking it from all angles at the two gum trees which always stood as my goals, get it through and into the dairy paddock. You could practice kicking from 40/30/20 degree angle also varying distance from goals and able sometimes to get it over from fifty feet out marked approximately with "Bix" yardstick tape measures being a thing we didn't have so I'm not sure how accurate I was! I was imagining myself most days as Norm Smith or Percy Beames, Melbourne champions. Big stars of the day including the aforementioned were Jack Titus of Richmond, Dick Reynolds of Essendon, and Collingwood's Ron Todd, who I met years later in Deniliquin and was able to buy a beer.

Education, there wasn't much, school until thirteen on and off, helped on the farm, learnt to shoot a gun at Coglan's, skin rabbits, at home chop the wood, dig for fences or the night soil pit which had to be moved every few months this was hard yakka for a young lad, and on many occasions I would dig deep for a new pit only to find an old deposit. We, myself and Terry had to be up 5am milking the cows and separating the cream and milk this was done in a manual separator with a crank handle which was a boring job. The Old Boy there but often not much use again.

c.1938 we were chucked off the farm for non-payment of rent I imagine and went back to Tentertown which was hard for all of us as there was a diphtheria epidemic and rheumatic fever in Victoria as well as Polio. Terry tested positive on the swab for diphtheria and spent four months at Infectious Diseases ward on the Glenister road about a mile out of town, six Nissen huts, and Terry said to me years later it was very basic accommodation. You weren't allowed to go too near but Mum would take me I would stand outside the fence and talk to Terry and I threw him a footy over. Of course Terry he was hopeless at all ball sports and would hardly ever play footy with me, I used to bribe him with a toy bob or a halfpenny to make him play but he couldn't even kick it, it was almost always a banana. What he wanted to do was sit there for hours mooning or drawing, he drew castles and 18th century gents with wigs he loved all that, like Captain Cook in the button coats, he once drew them in his copybook at school and was caught red-handed and given the cuts by Sister Dorothea an old sadist if ever there was one. Mistakes would get a fast ruler on the forehead or she would pull the ear and twist it. No counselling in those days!

c. 1942 I struck out on my own working as shearer and roustabout in country NSW travelled by buggy to Wia Wia then train to Strathmorgan then buggy again to Hulme, a distance of 240km where Joe Coglan was waiting for me. A bit teary that first day after working at "Braebrook" Station 7:30am-10am, then ten minute break not a second more, then lunch was sandwiches from 12:30-1 then we went till 5:30pm, tea in those days was mutton or a stew, breakfast was eggs or mutton fry and black tea. Cooks were very proud and difficult people for some reason though they had nothing to do compared to the shearers they would quit on the smallest complaint, Joe tried to make me do it but I said "no way." I went for the blade working up to sometimes more than one hundred sheep in a day, not bad for a young fella. Stan Gallagher the flaming redhead was the best shearer at "Braebrook," even Mr Robertson boss man of the Station would give Bluey a Saturday morning off to go to the races at Pennoth, such was the favour held by this star of the sheds. I accompanied Bluey to Pennoth on several occasions sometimes betting only a few shillings for a £20 return. Meanwhile brother Terry blew out of Tentertown took the train to Melbourne to stay with Auntie Vi at 61 Campbell St, Prahran where he was well coddled by Vi who I got to know well in later years. Vi was quite a character herself and what was then known as a "cupboard smoker," cigarette smoking not being approved of for ladies she would lie in the hearth of her bedroom fireplace and blow the smoke up the chimney! Vi never married but longstanding rumour had her in a friendship of a secret nature with Father O'Neil in Prahran, he would visit her at Campbell St on Sundays after 11 o' clock mass and then be back in church for the afternoon service! Mary Halloran a great friend of Vi's told me years later that Vi was forbidden from Father's funeral by the parish ladies of St Dominics who had always had it in for her.

Younger readers would find it surprising how much sway was held by superstition and the Catholic Religion, and in other areas by Protestants though we didn't have much to do with them. Evidently many Catholic priests in Tentertown, Hillitt, Glen Close, Ballarat, Geelong and later I found in Melbourne areas were big drinkers and very hypocritical in other ways as shown well by the Father O'Neil example. I recall in Corio Father Gerard Byrne having to remove himself in great haste because local lad Tim Pirrie's father Bert said Father Byrne took his son into the vestry and did something to him but it was all hushed up of course and in those days you didn't question. This is some years later when Bill Riordan and I were starting to get some good business going around Corio, sometimes with the Corio council, buying up land from the Church they didn't want, and Bill used to tell me quite a bit about the darker corners of the diocese. This is Bill Riordan later a very successful publican in Corio, Cheshire St, and a very good businessman then Mayor of Geelong, 1967-8.

By c. early 1950s I had begun to court Margaret Ellen Brearley and we were duly married at St Francis Xavier Russell Park Geelong April 30 1954 with baby Cheryl appearing in 1956 in time for the Melbourne Olympics. We had ten happy years at 7 Ellsmore Rd selling in 1964 getting a £4000 return on a £2300 initial investment which was a good result. Baby Suzanne joined the family in 1960 by this time I was clearing blocks in West Geelong and doing a nice sideline in bricks and building equipment in business with Frank Teleki. Frank was a Hungarian New Australian and great bloke who's grasp of English was unfortunately always destined to remain a work in progress! But Frank got what he wanted alright and I was able to learn in business from him. We went onto the Lanro arcade in West Geelong in 1962 as full partners. That was my first land purchase with contract to build, a big step up for me. We went on to land acquisition and development projects in Geelong, Tullamarine Airport redevelopment 1978-9, and development project in Puck St, Essendon Gardens with Westron, a global firm. I bought Frank out on his retirement in 1980 in July 1985 I was attaining land acquisition rights to develop Corio waterfront picked up the phone to speak to the contract land surveyor and found it was Frank's son Adrian! I have seen him several times since then and wife Anita.

My father as referenced having passed away in 1957 after lingering in Geelong Hospital, was buried in Geelong General Cemetery visited sometimes by Mum and sometimes by me, Terry surprisingly never visiting saying he preferred to sit in his garden!

Terry chose to live his own lifestyle in Melbourne with his wife Judy, Terry working as secretary at the Melbourne Technical College later Royal Melbourne Institute of Technology eventually rising to become faculty secretary, a senior position. No contact for many years but then made contact five years ago after Judy's passing away he was set up in a unit paid for by me in Tollington Ave Glen Iris, until he had a couple of falls, moving to a smaller unit 13 Flagg Court, Carnegie which I set up with ambulatory aids, non slip surfacing, shower rail, etc., until he found accommodation at Grace McKellar not far from the ward Mum had been in years ago.

Visit to Terry on 22.8 three weeks ago, found him near elevator doors in ground floor foyer of B ward, in from the main car park. Able to identify me as family but do not know if he knew I was his brother. Which is a testimony to the Alzheimer's disease which had overcome him to some extent although he remained in good spirits. Sat with him there in foyer, no chance of getting him to the room I thought, so we talked for 20 mins or so but he distracted by operation of elevator doors and asked me several times what they were, etc. But he in good spirits, good colour & not distressed, I gave him the butterscotch and a shirt. Told on next visit 24.8 arrival 8:45am that Terry had died ten minutes before at 8:35. I stayed and saw him, he looked alright.

I remain in good health, some scare last year with high blood pressure spike and angina, 3 day admission to hospital for tests but that is all. Last surviving member of my immediate family. Married 48 years, my wife Margaret Ellen passed away after short illness & treatment for cancer at Peter MacCallum Institute, 30.5.02. Two children, five grandchildren, eight great grandchildren as of October 2014, latest little Zoe Alicia born 12.1.14.

I am glad I was able to reconnect with my brother after some years of estrangement.

Vale Terence Francis O'Connell 1926-2014
Son of Daniel Vance and Lillian Mary
Brother of Jack

NATHAN AND JORDAN

Do you know what though? Nathan's *mum* is good. She's really good. I even said it to him, I'm like, your mum is really nice. And Nath, he just sits there. And like, I know you're not gonna say your *own mum* is good. But I can say she is, even though it sounds pretty weird. I *know* it's weird, but I just think she's proof that a mum can really be good. So good. So good.

Their house is sort of weird. The inside is heaps nicer than outside. Like, *heaps*. I don't know how they can be rich because there's no dad, I don't know where the dad is, but they have like, golden stuff, golden tables and they have this TV that is a Ultra HD, it's really big. And their carpet is all everywhere and they have a *good* couch. It's like, *black*. And the only rule she has, Nathan's mum, is that when we have tea we have to have it in the kitchen area and sit up and watch TV together, but every other time she lets us be by ourselves in the TV room and watch the big TV. And she brings us the *nicest* stuff to eat. And she brings it all in from the car even though she's really fat. How nice is that? And she is *massive*. She wears these trackies, these bright yellow trackies, or really bright red, and when she comes towards you it's like, woah, that is so much trackie. She's like a *bed*. Like, massive fluoro bed. And she has big funny eyes, like starey. She is weird looking. But she's really generous, she's like a really generous person. When she comes in with the bags she's always really happy and she always goes, I got you kids somethin yummy! And she does this like little song for us, like a chant, she goes:

> *Yummy, yummy, yummy*
> *Yummy, yummy, yummy*
> *Yummy, yummy, yummy*

And she always does this sort of massive little *dance*, like with her hands up, dance. And she wants me and Nath to do it too. And we do, sort of. I *know* she's weird. But she, she showed us this thing, on the table, she put this massive thing of ice-cream, like a tub but longer, and it was Sammy D's Double Chocolate Magnifico Supreme Indulgence. Not bad. Not bad. And she's gonna get us the Cookies and Cream Indulgence. We saw the ad for it, Cookies and Cream, the one where the kids surf on the mountain and the mountain is all cream and out of

the mountain all cookies explode. And this other time
she brought us like two whole things, like two whole big
packs of Dimini's Homestyle Pizza Bites, the Mega Meat
Lovers ones, O my God. Nath gets to put them in the oven
and everything and he brought them in the TV room and
we got like thirty Bites *each*. O my God. With every Bite
you get like five Mega Meats, you get like salami, bacon,
sausage pieces, and beef and chicken tenders. Plus we got
separate Texas BBQ dipping sauce. And she showed us,
Nathan's mum, what she does is she gets the tenders off
and she puts the cheese around them so she's making like
a cheesy meat hot dog and I did that, I put my dog in the
dipping sauce and that is the best thing ever, O my God,
that sauce, it's *so tasty*, the way I was doing it, I was loving
it, I was like keeping on down in the little plastic thing,
like right down to get like the *tiniest* last bit of sauce, it
was like, *uughh*, the flavour, O fuck I said to Nath, this is
intense. And then after a while I felt sort of sleepy I fully
had a sleep right there. I just like flopped out on the black
couch and it was so nice, I slept for *ages.*

I know sometimes I should maybe, I should just go
home to my house, my mum. I will. I will it's just I want
to be here for a while. Nathan's mum she doesn't call me
Jordan she calls me Little One, that's her name for me.
The first time I like even met her she goes to me what's
your favourite chocolate bar and I went Force bars and

she opened her hand and one was there! She does stuff like that all the time. And sometimes I'm like, it's so weird, all this luckiness I'm having now, is, it's *because* of Force bars, like the weird thing of them, because, a kid at school I didn't even really know, Nathan, we were just in this boring *class* and he sees me having a Force bar and he goes to me do you want half of my Force bar? And I was like, OK. And then later he goes to me you should come to my house after school my mum has all these new Force bars. Like, new kinds. And to myself I was like, OK, he's a bit of a fatty and maybe he's being weird being all Mr Give Away Force Bars, but he's being nice to me, so, I don't know. I'll just go for a little while and have one Force bar. Or two, you can have two. And then I'll tell my mum later that I went to this new friend's house but not tell her I had Force bars and just make sure I eat enough of the stuff we always have for tea, otherwise she knows. One time I was on the way home and I had this whole big bag of Zip Chips secretly at like five-thirty and then at six I was supposed to have all these rissoles of hers, and she knew. But this time, I'll be like: control. So Nath and me we go to his house it's like out the back of school where the gap in the fence is and then you go through all this like dirt path and there's all these old trees on either side, it's fully like a forest. Except there's heaps of old chip packets and cans and crap, and I know that stuff is always everywhere but along that forest path bit there's like a *lot*. But then you come out the other side and Nathan's mum's house is just there, it's like all little and white. And it's nice, it looks nice on the outside but then I got closer to it like where the door is, and O my God.

She used to do this thing where you go to the door like just the front door to go in, and there's all these Force bars, just there! All these new choc wafer ones with marshmallow, they're new and nobody else has even had them yet and they're just there next to the mat. And soon I'm like ringing the doorbell and I've already had one, or more, they're not that big, and then she answers and I'm still eating them, I go hello like *hwmhwoo*! And I don't get in trouble, she laughs! She thinks it's hilarious. I go hi like *mwa*! And she just like does a bit of her dance. She's a *idiot*. One day she gave me a *hug*. It was like, ooo, ooo, that is too much trackie, aaa! But she's nice. She really likes me. She gave me a Berry Fruit Bomb and she goes don't tell your mum! And I'm like, I won't! And I wouldn't! No way! And now she puts Berry Fruit Bombs in the hall on the carpet so you can just eat them as you go along! And Muffin Chocs! And Zip Chips! All different things! O my God. Nathan can't *move*. He's getting *so* fat! I have to bring the stuff to him! I'm in the hall eating stuff *and* tryna carry some *and* put more in my pockets for him! Or me! Or me *and* him. It doesn't matter, there's so much, all these packets and packets of stuff! It's like the house is a supermarket! Like, exactly! And now she puts the stuff in even more places! She puts X-Crush in the *toilet*. On top of the top bit, they're there, so when you have a piss you're just like *staring* at them. There's like a line: Fresh X, X-Bolt, Blu X-Treme, she always changes what kinds. At first I didn't want to drink any of them because I thought it was sort of dirty to have a big drink in the toilet. But they're there. She puts them there already cold. They're nice. Why shouldn't we have a nice drink? You don't have to obey some dumb *rule* about when you should have things. So now I'm like standing in the toilet and I'm drinking and pissing at the same time, holding the can and my dick! It's like *continuous* coming in and going out it's the *weirdest* feeling it's like O my God there's no like stop to how much I can have.

But it's good that she's putting in this new one, Monster X-Treme, because the others were starting to get a bit boring. And I wish sometimes, like, Nathan's mum, she'd stay with me a bit more and say more things to me. I don't know. All she does is say all the time that I look really hungry and then she brings me more snacks. Anyway I *told* her, I *said* I don't want the X-Treme I'm sick of it, why can't we have something *new*? And she goes it's really good, I'm getting to be a big boy and she's happy with me and I can have like more responsibility.

So I have like a new thing now where I'm helping her, Nathan's mum. It's weird cause Nathan isn't even here anymore, there's this other new kid called Brendan. He's nice but he's pretty small. Like, skimpy. So I'm helping, I'm like learning to do the cooking. I'm allowed go in the kitchen and I can do the microwave and I can decide what to have and I've got like all these ideas about how to make things even better. Like with the Cheesy Potato Jewels, you can do them in the microwave but you can also do them in the oven at the end and that makes them even more crispy. So like, microwave *and* oven. Do the oven at the end, for like maybe *five* minutes. That's like, my special tip. Because, if you do that, then all the little crispy bits on the outside of the Jewels they will become really brown and then the whole thing will be like, extra crispy, and inside all the cheese will be even more totally melted. And then, you can get the other one with the best cheese that is really melty, which is Jimmy J's Three Cheese Potato Gems, the Gems, not the Jewels, and when you cook them, the Gems, you sort of have to do the opposite, you do them first in the oven and then do them in the microwave. But you should do them in the microwave for maybe just like, a tiny minute, and then the cheese will be more liquidy and will fully just *slide* out of the potato thing and into your mouth. But, be careful, because the cheese, that's white liquid, that's still really hot, and you can fully burn your tongue, so you should just like wave them in the air, wave them in the air like still on the plate, because, that will cool them even though you can drop them, I've dropped them. The other night I was in the kitchen and I dropped them on the floor and one went under the fridge like in the gap *under*, and so I was like reaching but it was sort of hard to get down, I am sort of bigger now. And Nathan's mum was there, and I was looking back at her, and she was doing her chant like even faster:

> *Yummy, yummy, yummy*
> *Yummy, yummy, yummy*
> *Yummy, yummy, yummy*

and I was trying! I was trying to get that snack, my fingers were like reaching almost there, *nearly* there, and then I *got* it. I *got* it. And then still on the floor I ate it. And she was laughing *so* loud. And then, I don't know, I just really suddenly wanted my mum. But then Nathan's mum, she picked me up and she just gave me the biggest smile and the biggest, *biggest* hug.

FOOTY MYSTERIES

NEW from Challenge Publishing and Bob Bottom

FOUR MORE EXCITING FOOTY MYSTERIES

Brothers and Footy Investigators Scotty Moran and Wayne "Forensics" Moran are on the case ... But how will the FOOTY MYSTERIES be solved?

Two Draft Picks to Midnight

Number six national AFL draft pick ace defender Dale Brin and number eleven pick gun forward Brenton Mulvaney are both offered lucrative contracts at Richmond, and both boys go on to enjoy some well-deserved celebrations at "Broadway," a high-class eatery and bar at Crown Casino. Only after leaving "Broadway" do they realise something is wrong – very wrong. Pausing briefly on Kings Way to buy a sausage roll, the talented eighteen-year-olds discover their wallets are missing. At AFL headquarters, Commissioner Allan Callett places a call to crack investigators Wayne "Forensics" Moran and his younger brother and venue/street activity expert, Scotty Moran. Scotty's intensive overnight assessment of the CCTV footage reveals both boys appear to be in possession of their wallets on arrival at "Broadway" and no wallets appear to have fallen from them during the six and a half hours the boys spent at the upscale eatery and bar. Therefore, the wallets must have been dropped somewhere at Southbank or possibly on the Kings Way Bridge. Media interest is building. Decisions will have to be made. Focussing in on the key facts, Wayne "Forensics" Moran posits that any cash will be long gone, but it is still possible to save the boys the hassle of getting all their cards again. But can the missing wallets be found? Should the boys cancel all the cards now, or wait until tomorrow?

$29.99   ISBN 978122437877   330 pages.

The Mystery of the Sleeping Mascot

North Melbourne mascot operator/performer Andrew Loy has spent hundreds of hours inside a large foam kangaroo and never had a problem – until now. Seconds into the round three half-time festivities at Etihad Stadium, Andy finds himself battling to stay awake, and at three-quarter time must again fight off the urge to become immediately insensate. Round five, he falls asleep at the opening bounce. Round six, he's out before the game even starts, dropping snout-first into the banner just as the boys were about to run through. Is it ventilation? Has the composition of the suit changed? AFL Commissioner Callett brings in crack investigators Wayne "Forensics" Moran and younger brother and air-flow expert Scotty Moran, the said Scotty wasting no time at all in commencing an exhaustive series of intothermal and oxygenic evaluations. Blood cell analysis reveals nothing. Respiratory penetration is normal. Scotty confesses himself baffled. By round eight, Andy has to be continuously held up by two buxom Kangarettes. North Melbourne fans are demanding answers. The *Herald-Sun* is on Andy's door, 24/7. The AFL says money is no object. Wayne "Forensics" Moran is a man who invariably knows where to focus. But can Wayne find a way to keep "Kanga" awake?

$29.99 ISBN 978122437878 378 pages.

The Case of the Missing Goal Umpire

AFL goal umpire Trever Wenn is due in the rooms two hours before the 1:10 pm bounce on game day – but at 11:05 am he is nowhere to be found. AFL Commissioner Allan Callett orders crack footy investigator Wayne "Forensics" Moran and transport/personnel logistics expert Scotty Moran into the AFL rapid-response helicopter to assess the situation. Scotty computes all possible routes along Punt Road or Williams Road while Wayne, with his trademark focus, makes contact with Umpire Wenn's good lady wife via her landline. Mrs Wenn says Umpire Wenn left their Beaumaris home at 10:15 am. Is he stuck in traffic? What are the contingency plans if a goal umpire is missing on the day? Who failed? Whose heads will roll? And what is Umpire Wenn's mobile number?

$29.99   ISBN 978122437879   444 pages.

In the Valley of Mick

Footy Investigators Wayne Moran and Scotty Moran fly to Arizona, USA, and the Collingwood Football Club's high-altitude performance/training camp, after disturbing reports that a figure resembling former coach Mick

Malthouse has been sighted repeatedly on the perimeters of the camp, standing immobile for hours, and staring fixedly at the players. But when the players attempt to draw closer, this figure cannot be located. Is it Mick? Or is it a fence paling or road sign? Are the boys maybe training too hard? Collingwood Football Club president Eddie McGuire says money is no object as visual assessment expert Scotty Moran begins an arduous analysis of every player's bio-optic capacity, while Wayne "Forensics" Moran, with the focus that has indeed become his trademark, vows to remain himself on the fence line for as long as it takes, telling president McGuire, "No one's going anywhere."

$29.99   ISBN 978122437880   701 pages.

ALSO AVAILABLE:

Appointment in Fremantle
ISBN 978122437882
The Fitness Trainer Who Came in from the Cold
ISBN 978122437883
Goodnight, Western Bulldogs
ISBN 978122437884
Tinker, Tailor, Soldier, Assistant Coach
ISBN 978122437885

AND

A Thousand and One Nights in Adelaide
ISBN 978122437886

AND 'The Geelong Trilogy'
ISBN 978122437226 *Cat Got Your Season Ticket*
ISBN 978122437227 *Cat on a Hot Stadium Roof*
ISBN 978122437228 *A Cat Only Has Nine Million in Cash Reserves*

MANDS '88

My Year Twelve subjects I did were Business Studies, Legal Studies, and Geography. And English.

And Maths.

And running. I did running. And gym.

The first time I ever kissed a girl, it was Mands. That was in Year Eleven. And when I got home I looked at myself in the bathroom mirror to see if I looked different.

I was worried about the tongues when I was doing it but it was OK.

I kissed her again when we were on the front drive of her house after we went to see 'Good Morning, Vietnam'. I paid for the taxi to Waverley Cinema and back. I wanted it to be – I wanted to show her I liked her and that money didn't matter.

Just because I was fit and did running and weights, and I was captain of aths, and she was the hottest, very good-looking, like, the best-looking girl at school, everyone said we'd get together, but I didn't think so. I thought she liked Justin.

We went on our first real proper date to the Mi Li Chinese Restaurant in Waverley South. I liked that, it was good, they had a little round table on the table and the little table spun around. So if the sauce is over there, you can just *spin* it over. The Chinese restaurants I'd been to with Mum and Dad didn't have that.

Amanda had a Pepsi and I had a Diet Pepsi. I wanted to keep the can, but that's too much. 'First date can.'

Before that, the first kiss ever, that was at Bretty Medew's party. And we were in the corridor, we had a two-litre West Coast Cooler and we both had some. I did wear my singlet, that night, I did, cause I hoped she would be there. And in the corridor, we were there and she goes to me don't you even like me? And I was like, oh! I thought: *she wants me to kiss her now, I should kiss her now, like she's like asking me to, now, I should do it.* I was, it's just that – you don't think you can ever do it. Touch them. It's too incredible, they wear that dress and it's like, that, you just look from far away. Then you have your actual hand on her. I had my hands on like, her hips.

The song that was on when we kissed was INXS, 'New Sensation'. I always remember.

Her hair. Her hair is really good, beautiful. It's pretty long. And she's – she has. She's just very good-looking.

We did that thing for so long where you keep your jeans on but you try and root. With your jeans on. Lying on top of each other for a long time, so long, and kissing so much, and you push, push your jeans together. It's really frustrating. It feels nice. It's really frustrating.

I remember the first time when I first touched her vagina though. We were behind her house in her backyard, we were on the tan-bark area. We were kissing and she put my hand up right into her shorts leg, the leg of her shorts, which were big shorts, they were really baggy shorts, so lots of room, thank you, thank you big shorts. Even her leg, up there, just her leg is the best thing. I could touch all day, I could kiss all day, and touch her there, but, I went even further, all along up to her underpants, I felt the line, and the *hair*, we were pashing so much, I lifted up the side of her undies, and went in, I went under and – and *in*, and it was just – incredible. I was just. I mean – surprised. And the thing I always remember, I was so surprised because, there was liquid. In there. I thought it would be like the inside of a glove, just like warm and really soft. I didn't imagine any liquid. The liquid was a surprise, that it was wet. Sorry. This is just my dumb way of saying that it was even more incredible and good than I imagined.

Sorry.

One day I felt mean because I wanted to root her so much in her room, and she was really ready to, but her little brother came to the door. He was like knocking, I opened it like one tiny little bit and looked at him and said to him, I was like: *go AWAY!!!* I must have looked crazy.

When she's not at school she wears big shorts, like linen, and nice shirts and jumpers, and shoes with these little nut things on top, or fringes. The shoes, it's interesting with the shoes. That's different. All that stuff's cause her family is richer than mine.

And the olives. Fancy bread. All that stuff.

Her mum and dad are nice to me though. Her mum is. Her dad is, too. He's Anthony. She's Sonya. He works for a computer company. I'm not really sure what she does. Even after this long, I'm still embarrassed. They have me for dinner. And in my head, I'm like: thank you for feeding me so I can root your daughter.

Sometimes I expect them to go really suddenly, like to me, at the table: *what are you doing?!! get out!! get out!!*

Sometimes in her room we lie down and we just look at each other. I like just trace her nose, like really gently.

She has the best nose. Or lie there and I say: shut your eyes. And kiss her eyelids.

Amanda. Amanda. Amanda. Amanda.

Her best friend is Rebecca. Becs. And I always knew, I knew in that way that you do that I had to beat Becs, like win against her. Like Mands was going to like me more than Bec, I had to do that. Like, make sure. But you have to be not obvious about it. Be really nice to Bec. Never say anything against Bec. Just say: we'll go really soon to Bec's place, for sure, really soon. But let's just stay here and snuggle for a bit.

And I do fitness, man. And buy tops. New t-shirts. New singlets.

And I buy her stuff. Mands. I bought her the pendant with the emerald in it. It was a lot of money but I don't care. It was 280 bucks, but I'm glad. You have to spend that much to get something that's not crap. And I got her a notebook, and nice paper and a pen. But it was pretty good, the emerald, that was the best. When I gave her the little box and the card.

You always have to think of stuff to do. On the weekends. Every weekend, you have to have something. You have to *do* stuff. Movies. I always look at what movies are on.

After four months Mands said to me at the Waverley skate park: sometimes I think about us breaking up. She didn't really *want* to, but just sometimes she just *thought* about it. And I felt like, I couldn't believe it. I felt sick in my guts. Then I walked home from Waverley South to Rinnon. It took me like two hours.

I made her cry and apologise. That's not true: she was already crying. But I made her do it more. That was the afternoon at my house. In my head I was like: *stay upset. I can't just let her come back so easily.*

At the start, when we were just starting to do it, sex, like really sex all the way – I'm not, I don't know. I think of myself on top of her, on the floor in her room, next to her little wooden desk. I hope I was OK. Or as good as I should have been. I think I was OK. We were both not that great but we kept trying.

The first time we had sex all the way I didn't even come. I was so – I don't know, whatever I was – that I didn't even remember that you did, that that was what you did when you finished. I think I was so shocked to finally have my cock in there and like really be doing it I just moved for twenty minutes and then I just *stopped*. But then later we were doing it again and I had this incredible like electric feeling all up and then really at the tip of my cock, *so* much more than when you do yourself, like by yourself, the whole feeling was so incredible and I pulled out and looked down and saw at the end of the condom there was this white blob there. And out loud I just went – not even to her, or myself, I don't know who – I just went – 'oh my God!'

I'm getting better now. Mands can have orgasms with me inside or just with my fingers. With my fingers, you do it, you stop and then start again. You *wait*. You be really delicate. But then also when we're having full-on sex and Mands starts coming, I just *hold on*, man, all the way through. I'm getting good. One time she had the biggest one, because we were kind of on our sides in my bed, which is pretty narrow, so we were kind of up against the wall but she was like a little more along the wall than me, so I was kind of fucking sort of from below and up, it was like a new angle, this sidey and *up* one. And we did that, and we did that, I gave *more* and she like tremble tremble shiver shivered. *Big* tremble shivers. I was like: good? More? And she was like: oo. ooo.

It's not like I don't get some good ones. That time, on the couch in her lounge room, I thought my whole dick was going to explode.

I'm just lucky. Everyone wants to know everything, like, at school. Juzzy does. But I just shut the fuck up.

Only a couple of us at school are even a couple. Me and Mands. Brett and Jessica. Pooles and Sares.

And our school, which is really Catholic, it's terrible. They tell you that a rapist can't give a lady a baby because the lady contracts and that – stops it. Mr Martin told us that, in R.E., in Year Ten. That's not true. This friend of Mands' mum said that's not even true. And in Year Eleven this couple who were a married couple came and talked to the whole year like the entire year assembly about how they never did it till they got married. Of course I just looked at them for the whole assembly and was imagining them doing it. He, the husband, he was kind of little and bony. And she wasn't very nice. Bigger than him. And then, at another whole year assembly, Mr Sheehan said all these things about George Michael, and 'a certain song', which we all knew was 'I Want Your Sex' and Mr Sheehan goes George Michael has no respect for women, and he is a very poor role model, and if we really thought about the example that George Michael is sending out to young people, we would see he is not a proper role model for our community. And this girl called Jane Cowan got up we were all on these plastic chairs, but she stood up in front of hundreds of kids and the teachers and everything and said that George Michael was good and they shouldn't be telling us he was bad, and it was up to *us* to decide whether we liked him or not. And us Year Elevens, like the whole year, we all started clapping. That – that was the biggest most rebellion we ever had.

Still. It's a bit sad to leave, I guess. But I'm really looking forward to uni. Mands is doing Arts at Melbourne because she wants to get into Law. And I'm doing Business Studies at Deakin. But we'll still get to see each other every day. And then we'll have to wait a couple more years, and then, I'm going to ask her to marry me. Sometimes we talk about our kids. We want to have two,

two kids. Mands has names for them. I don't know about some of the names, just between you and me. She wants, for a girl: Sasha. And if it's a boy, for a boy she really wants to call it Oliver.

THE ANZAC SPIRIT

CRAIG COTTER: Well, obviously Callum Loake as editor, he's a new cultural fit for us, and we've acknowledged that. Callum's come up from more of a marketing background, communications background, and he's made a really significant contribution in those areas, with a youth approach and a more aggressive approach —

INTERVIEWER: But that, that's not —

CRAIG COTTER: Neil, what I'm not denying, and I say this to everyone listening, is that on this occasion he did make an error of judgement in the heat of the moment and a judgement that was not correct.

THE LAST ANZACS?
A NEW generation of a few brave warriors is keeping the Anzac tradition alive in the Middle East, while numbers

of Anzac veterans continue to tragically dwindle here at home.

Sun-Mail 24/4

It started TEN minutes late! But now it's amazing. #dawnservice

CRAIG COTTER: Obviously a lot of people were upset by the graph, and doing a graph, any sort of graph, in any form, showing any projected decline in veteran numbers, living veteran numbers, was obviously not a correctly judged decision. And I think Callum has a lot of reflecting to do, and this has caused him stress, and he and his family have suffered a great deal of stress. But he's a very talented young man, and while his choice of story on this occasion was poor, I think he will take that on the chin and I think this will be a very significant learning experience for him going forward.

Given your stance perhaps you will be very happy when Australia has become an Islamic republic!

Keith, Wynett

I say to you people that the veterans of Iraq and Afghanistan will continue to march even if no-one comes to see them.

Diggers4Ever

TO THE *SUN-MAIL*: The Anzac spirit will survive your dishonest, dishonorable, disgraceful attack.

True Blue, Kepp Point

CRAIG COTTER: Well, obviously it was Callum himself who made the decision to run a story like that on the front page, and the editorial, and that was a mistake, and he has come forward and indicated that to the board. But what I would just say, Tony, is that witch-hunts conducted against any one individual seem to me to be pretty unhelpful at this stage.

Incredible to reflect on the amazing history of our country. #dawnservice

TO 'TRUE BLUE' (*SUN-MAIL* 26/4): Isn't Mr Loake entitled to his opinion? And isn't the best defence against

growing Muslim extremism surely to defend our wonderful diversity?
Robyn, Jerillee

For all those who think it's a trumpet it is actually called
a BUGLE. #dawnservice

THE PRIME MINISTER: Yes, yes I did. And in terms
of attacking the Anzac tradition in this country, I was
just very surprised that anyone would do that.

CRAIG COTTER: Obviously on the graph, Virginia,
we've always said that was insensitive and I strongly
condemn it, I condemn it in the strongest possible terms,
and it's the sort of thing that should never have even been
considered as news.

but you notice no one marches for wars of the nineteenth
century right
ribbit23
Share/Flag/Like

i think that kids should do it even if all the old people are gone because its tradition :)
kaylaG
Share/Flag/Like

why do we even have to care about this
diDo45
Share/Flag/Like

is gallipoli even in australia
diDo45
Share/Flag/Like

hey diDo45 we could be being invaded right now and you wouldnt know FAIL
duffbear
Share/Flag/Like

What the minority will never understand is that the Anzac spirit lives on in the hearts and minds of ALL Australians.
Russell, Sinnon Park

INTERVIEWER: So do you know how many Anzac veterans are currently still alive?

CRAIG COTTER: I'm not even going to get into that, Jon. I think it's offensive to even start to do that sort of calculation, obviously.

INTERVIEWER: Did you think the story was wrong?

THE PRIME MINISTER: Mate, I thought it was disgusting.

this year instead of watching the footy like everyone else I went bowling. you know in respect of the fallen
skeetjosh99
Share/Flag/Like

I think we should have a day for other people not just anzacs
hollyk
Share/Flag/Like

hey I killed some turkish people
boomb
Share/Flag/Like

Now Mr Loake is being hounded by the media dogs and is pleading to be left alone. Isn't it time to stop blaming the victim and confront the fact that depression in the workplace is a significant factor in our community?
Heather, Toonang North

Irrespective of what you think about this war, or that war, or any war, Anzac Day is not the time to question the commitment of the individuals who gave their lives and that is where our thoughts should always be.
Colin, Yerrondale

CRAIG COTTER: My point is that obviously Callum is suffering from an illness and this is more an occasion for concern than anything else.

- Pressure has been positive.
- Forced to become more proactive.
- Fresh look at our subscription base.
- Getting out more free copies.
- Finding those high-repeat pick-up spots.
- Out of adversity, that's when you learn.
sunmail_pres_distrib_mmg.ppt

He targeted the old. The most vulnerable. And that is what is unforgivable.

Gary, Calabra

CRAIG COTTER: It's always been pretty obvious to us that there is a line, with respect to our values, and if you work for us, and it becomes apparent that you've stepped over that line, then there is no place for you, you will be condemned as is appropriate and you will be removed. And that is our commitment to the community.

There's always one, isn't there?

Don, Gap Hill

MEDIA STATEMENT MR CALLUM LOAKE

All enquiries: kierann@tptcomms.com.au

I understand that the stories and editorial which appeared in the *Sun-Mail* on Anzac Day, and which were commissioned by me as editor, and for which I take complete and sole responsibility, have caused deep pain and distress to many persons in the community.

Today, I say unequivocally: I am sorry. I apologise

for the hurt and distress that I have caused. I apologise to the Australian and New Zealand Army Corps veterans of World War One, World War Two, the Korean War, the Emergency Operation in Malaya, the Vietnam War, the First and Second Iraq Wars, and the War Against Terrorism in Afghanistan. I would also like to additionally apologise to all of their families and loved ones, and to anyone else who was offended or adversely affected by any of the stories that I published. I would also like to apologise to APCP Media Partners and the directors and shareholders of Congon Limited.

I have for some time been suffering from a significant stress and depression-related condition. I am now receiving the appropriate care at the appropriate institutions. I would like to take this opportunity to thank the doctors, nurses and staff at The Groves Private Hospital, who do such a fantastic job and have given me and my family so much wonderful care and are just total professionals.

This has been an important time for me to reflect on what really matters. My wife and my two boys have been incredibly supportive and understanding of me, and if there's one thing I've learned through this whole experience it's that the most important thing in the world is family.

My dad, who suffered from chronic back pain all his life, taught me to always stand up and admit when I did something wrong. And that is what I have done today. I hope, after an appropriate period, to rejoin the community in a responsible lead role within the news media. But the journey for me now is very much about understanding the past, looking to the future, and healing.

THE POOFTER BUS

It comes every day and it waits just over there.

What do you reckon? It's *pink*.

It's really big and gay. It's a really big bus and it's pink
and it's gay and it has *heaps* of room in it.

But the driver is just this little guy who's like a dwarf.
A tiny *little* poofter.

THINGS THAT WILL GET YOU ON IT

Reading books.
Listening to olden music where there is a lot of violins.
Not even knowing who the best fast bowler for Australia
is.
Those shoes, because of the purple bit.

Not even knowing who Ian Healy is.

Not even knowing who Dermott Brereton is!

Not even knowing who won the Brownlow this year. Year before that. Year before that.

Watching movies where it's all talking.

Wearing a *cardigan.*

Wearing anything weird.

Doing anything weird.

Being a poofter.

MORE RULES

Sometimes you're not a poofter but then you are one because of just one thing.

Like you can be friends with us, and then we find out you have that hat which has a koala on it.

Or that you went to *gymnastics.*

Plus here in your room you have this bookmark, with a drawing of *Sovereign Hill.*

And you go: that's just a picture of Sovereign Hill, my family, we went there.

But that just means probably your *dad* is a poofter.

Maybe your whole family is poofters.
Two poofter dads and they made you.
A whole family of poofters.
From *Sovereign Hill*.

Other times it's not even one thing, it's just that all of you
is just really, really poofterish. You know?
It's like, everywhere in you. Like even normal stuff looks
poofter on you. Or becomes poofter. That ruler. Is now a
poofter ruler. And your bag is a poofter bag.
That's the worst. Then you have to go get the poofter
bus every day.

EVERY DAY

Poofter ruler. Poofter bag. Poofter pencil-case. Poofter
water bottle. Poofter books, obviously. Poofter folder,
poofter pen, poofter textas, poofter writing, the writing
that is the writing of a poofter. Poofter shoes, poofter
socks. Poofter shoelaces, the shoelaces that only a poofter
would have. Poofter lunch, poofter *sultanas*. Poofter drinks.
Poofter pizza, which is the kind of pizza you want. Poofter
clothes. Poofter pants, poofter *bathers*. Poofter holiday
house, that you go to. See all the pictures of it in a poofter
magazine. Poofter street. Poofter *countries*. Poofter car,
poofter plane, poofter bike, poofter *helicopter*. Poofter bus.

THE ACTUAL BUS

The poofter bus is full of miserable poofters holding on to each other and crying. Or they're like really tired. Exhausted from being such poofters.

NOT POOFTER

Lollies that are good. Chips.
Footy.
Some TV shows.

TO SHEL,
MOSTLY ABOUT MUM

Shelly. This is your sister. Pick up your phone. Shel. Shel. Well, call me when you can about *Mother's Day*, and listen: Mum's *new ideas*.

So did you talk to Mum? Did she tell you about *Wendy?* Oh well, he's left her. Oh yes. After all that. His operation. Everything. And he's up, he's out of the hospital, and *she* always thought he had a thing for the woman next door. I know. And she confronted him she said oh, you're very fond of Margo. And he says oh, she's an interesting woman, interesting to talk to, I'm allowed to talk to people, leave me alone. All this. And then he's sat her down and said I'm leaving you. I'm leaving you for Margo. Wendy says how long has this been going on? He says it's not physical. It's not a physical relationship. *Bullshit*, Mum says. Hey? Oh yes, they've moved in together. Somewhere else. And the husband's still there, her husband, Margo's husband. And then Wendy. Still neighbours. No! I thought that too but *no,* because Wendy went to see a counsellor in Strathfield, and get this: she's *with the counsellor. Wendy.* I know! That's what I said to Mum! She says it *is* responsible because Wendy never paid. They just had a first session and she never paid. How bout that counsellor? Still. It's good for Wendy?

No, just the three days with them. Then they drove back and we stayed till the end of the week. Oh well, they both got into the drinks. Mum's very happy to get going about midday. We got home from shopping on the first day and she said to me what about a bubbles. I said, *Mum,* it's eleven a clock in the *morning.* And she said, oh, I thought because it's sunny. God knows what her and Dad get up to at home. They're probably starting up after breakfast. That's why they love the cruises. It's ten days of guilt-free drinking. She doesn't even go off to the sites, or whatever, the scenic places. She just stays on board. He told me. When they went to Hobart he traipsed round Port Arthur while she stayed the whole time in the Seafarers Bar. *Very* happy.

Oh, hello darlin. Oh, it was alright. No, at Mum and Dad's. Well, she just gets funny if there's a lot of chips and lollies before we eat. Oh, she *hates* it. She takes a basket of chips and hides it in the cupboard. In her pantry. We know she does it. And the kids are sitting there. Robbie just goes and gets them now. He says Lynne, where's the chips? And she's put them up there, you look up the top shelf, you can see the basket.

Hey Shel. We're in *Kmart.* Oh, towels. Towels, really. Well we went to this place that Mum wanted to go for cheap ones and she got some there. And now we're in Kmart and we're going to get a bath towel and a little washer, for Mia. And then Mum wants to go to Bed Bath and Table. Well that's *right*, that's very true isn't it? That's what I said to Mum. Mum, Shel says you can *never have enough towels*. Mum? Mum! Shel, Mum says she's not listening.

still in kmt 😖

not a bad idea

the cops would find her

yah covered in 50 towels 🔪🔪🔪🧻🧻🧻😬😬😬

I know. I know. I know. Hello. *And* getting her out of
the car. It'll be worse than her seventieth. I said to her,
Mum. Can't we go to the Emerald? I said you love it there.
And she says they've gone off it. She says to me her and
Dad went and she had loin of pork and it wasn't very
good. And Dad had the shashliks and he only got two,
you don't get enough. And it's too noisy. I said to her,
alright, you've been there a hundred times and you loved
it, but alright. Now it's Piccolo. She wants Piccolo. I said
you know it's thirty dollars. She said I know. I said to her
you know it's thirty dollars for a *parmigiana*. She said
well I never mind paying more if it's good. And that's
when I just had to put the phone down for a minute.

No, Mum's here. She won't go home, she's watching *The
Jewel Thief*. Well, she read the book. And she likes Pierce
Brosnan. *Mu-uuuu-um!* It's *Shel*. No? No. Shel? She'll call
you when it's over. Hey? Well it's *The Jewel Thief*, Shel.
I know. I know. Well, you can say that to her when you
talk to her later, can't you. Yes, yes. Bye, bye. Thank you.

God, I don't know. For Mum's Day? Have you got her
anything? Maybe a vase? I know. *Grog*. That'll do it.

So we're standing there and she says to Mum, oh no, she's my partner. Shoulda seen Mum's face. In the car I said to Mum, it's Bindi, I *told* you about Bindi and Leah. Though to be fair to Mum, she told Mum they had *four* kids, and I think Mum just got a bit flustered.

I got her a vase. And some chocolates. Which Mia put *in* the vase and now I'm worried Mum'll get her hand stuck in. What? Oh. Alright. Well, I'll ring you back later and tell you *the rest of that story*. What? Yeah, yeah. Love ya.

Listen, what do you think about Piccolo? For Mum's Day? No, Shel, I told you, they've got some vendetta against the Emerald. Or Mum says they do. They'll never go there again. I know. I know. And it's *us* paying. I don't really care but she'll be terrible on those stairs. I know. Anyway I booked it. For the Sunday. Shel. Shel. I just really need you to be with me on this one.

Oh god, I'm dreading it. The one I'll never forget is Trevi's, but she does it all the time, it's a *thing* now, everywhere we go, she's *on* the waitress, she gets so *crazy* at the waitress, we sit down and she says I don't think that girl's going to take our order and I'm like, Mum, fuckin hell, we just got here. And by the time they do come over Mum's givin her the Satan eyes. Oh god. Do you remember that poor fat girl at Trevi's? I thought Mum was gonna *hit* her. Over *bread rolls*. And then the manager comes and she *flirts* with him, god, that's what he wants, some seventy-one-year-old flirting at him. And Dad's there looking straight ahead, doing his ignoring.

Oh, I think she's been good. She said some nice things about Mia. Said that's a pretty dress. And Mia, bless her, she loved it. Came out on the patio and was very important.

Shelly. Shelly. Pick up. Pick up. Tell me when you and Jay are coming down. Mum is *calling me six times a day*.

Yes. Yes. Yes. Yes. Yes. Yes. Piccolo. Yes. At one. As god is my witness. I Will. See. You. There.

r u here?

u here yet? we're in the back.

Ok. Pls hurry I cant have more bourbon 😩 😩 😩

I'd say a 9

out of 10

yah 💀

Shel. Shel. Shel. Shel. I don't want to talk about Piccolo. Shel. Let's just let it go. It just. Shel. It never happened. There's no Piccolo, and we never went there. I'm working with that.

I saw Mum. Well she was a bit uppy with *me*. But then I remembered a few things I did say to her on Sunday, when we were getting her into the car.

No, but I saw *Dad* this morning. No, at their place. I took him to Bunnings then dropped him back. But oh, he's naughty to Mum. Oh, he is. I said to him, Robbie's got the trailer this weekend is there anything you want to get rid of? And he gestures towards *Mum*. With his thumb, at Mum. Oh, it *was* funny, he sort of got me by surprise and I did laugh. Poor Mum right there at the table. I said sorry Mum I didn't mean it. Poor old Mum. No wonder she has a sav blanc or two.

I mean, I hear you. Rob thinks she's worse. Still. I think she still has a bit of fun. Do you think? I think they're happy in their own strange way. They do watch the rugby together. It's their generation, it's that old sort of marriage, that, you know, people don't have anymore. Well, Mum does.

Yeah. I was thinking about what you said the other day. But *what*? I mean, at least he goes outside, you know. Once she's done the kitchen and her Sudoku and the other thing, her puzzle books, god. She's still got six hours till the news is on.

Oh god, don't talk about it, Shel. Please god, her first. He'll be alright. But her. I can't imagine it. Oh, I know. I know. I know. I shouldn't say that. Maybe she'd be alright. Have a cruise by herself. Be alright by herself. Enjoy the drinking.

JULIAN, 11 AM

– So I had a good week. I think.

– Mmm.

– It was fine. Issie, I took Issie to the movies, and I should say something about that. And work – I did work. I'm having some trouble coordinating myself, to do with work. I'm having some trouble, I had some trouble teaching, and I – I think, I'm aware that this is in some sense a ridiculous thing to say, I was thinking on the way down here that I *would* say this but it sounds so improbable – but I find, I found this week that teaching, I mean things at home too, yes, but now *teaching*, if I'm teaching, if I'm giving a lecture on the particular texts we're doing, I feel *sad*. Unusually sad. I'm aware that that sounds ridiculous. That I'm teaching these texts, these particular texts and I'm suddenly having this trouble. Extra trouble. That I'm in this trouble.

– What were the texts?

– Oh, Freud. Freud. Freud. Freud. We start with Freud. Well, we start with Saussure, and then Jakobson, we do some early semiology, some early-twentieth-century theory of language, language meaning, and that's really the theory before theory, in a sense; then psychoanalysis, and that's, this is week three, and we're really building up to phenomenology, Heidegger, the thought that really makes the theory, what we think of now *as* theory. But we do do Freud. We do some Freud.

And this, this goes to my – and, yes, I mean here we are and I know we've talked about this before and I know it's tedious to keep making objections to something one is also continuously participating in, but this – psycho-analysis, psychotherapy – I have objections to this which you know and which we've said, we've talked about, and you maybe don't need to hear again my *account* of this. Here. Today.

But I – what I still think is still maybe worth saying, is – and I don't know for sure if it's worth me making the objection or continuing to make the objection that this, all of this, in here, anything we *say*, anything I *say*, in here, in therapy, in analysis – I mean I think we should at least include the idea in here that this is a discourse like any other, and maybe making the basic mistake, the basic Western mistake, the same basic mistake of any Enlightenment thought system that thinks it can name or speak or control thought, *life,* in ways it just really *can't.* I mean I don't want to be too – but this is my work, which really is to think about these things, and I should say that this is Varls, a lot of this is Varls, who really is one of the better commentators on Derrida, this is Pierre Varls's claim that if you want to do philosophy now, if you want to *think* now, you have to say, that, that you cannot make a new and more fluid knowledge system and a new social and political system overnight, but what you *can* do is at least oppose the violence and exclusion of the existing system and its insistence that it has already marked, in its language, the limits of what is known, formulatable, *possible,* and that you *can* confront that existing, dominant, totalising system with gestures of indeterminacy, gestures of incompleteness, gestures of refusal. And that the promise of theory now, and really, the more critical part and better part and corrective part of the Western thought system for fifty, sixty years now, is that we really *can* learn this lesson and just *take in* a more radically destabilising complexity and reflexiveness and *be* less authoritarian and just stop thinking that we *know.* And I realise this can sound fanciful or pie-in-the-sky and of course a lot of people don't like this kind of thinking, and you may not like it, I mean, I'm not saying you, you're not necessarily saying that, but you could think that way, a lot of people do, some of my students do, but a lot of them *don't*, and when you look at what we're *in*, the system we're *in*, the idea of making something different doesn't look so completely insane.

But then – because, I mean – then, alright, I *do* have the problems, the fundamental problems that bother me *here*, right, which is what we've said is my anxiety and my depression and that I can't finish my papers and I *don't* do enough grant proposals and I just *need* to do some things so I can stay at the university which is the only place I've ever really felt at home, really, anywhere. I mean, I think it *is* possible to make small cells, small intellectual cells, outside the university; when Lenin and Krupskaya were in Zurich she baked and they lived in a very small house and they had to survive on remittances, very small amounts of money. But I think that that more independent scholarly life, intellectual life, is much more difficult in a place like Australia, which is further from larger intellectual circles – I mean, when we say Zurich, in the First World War, that was a centre of intellectual and émigré life at a time when the international socialist movement in a meaningful sense still existed and the Left was in a much, much healthier state than it is now. What we have now is a Left after a *century* of more capitalism and seeming capitalist success, even though that success is predicated upon stripping every more independent and scholarly vestige out of the old learning system, the university system, and out of *every other* system and getting to this world with nothing but more corporations, more advertising, more superficial surface activity to encourage consumption, and that's for the people who *can* be good consumers and the rest are simply going to be immiserated, or outcast, or interned. I know we've talked about this. But that's why we need to make our thought and our theory as rigorous as possible while we wait for a serious Left movement among working people and ordinary people to come back and that *will* happen, but it may take another fifty, or maybe another hundred and fifty years. In the meantime the start of I think a good life is to see that the main system, the consumption system, *is* in trouble, is *not* sustainable, really, and that is why we have to try and think in some sort of different way and get out of thought habits that are enormously destructive to ourselves and to the earth.

But this is – you asked, because – last week, you asked me why I'm so attached to Derrida, or: what did you say? Why do I *like* Derrida. Well I do *like* him. I do. I do. I read Foucault, I like Foucault, I like Lacan, but Derrida is the thinker I come back to again and again, I just, I think he is an amazing thinker, and I've been thinking about that: *why*, *why* do I think he is? And I think it's because with Derrida you can reach back and apprehend and interrogate the fundamental structures of meaning and of language in our civilisation and once you are there you have the chance to absolutely start again, begin again, and make an entirely new system, not today, but one day, and, as he says, as Derrida says, work for a future world that will 'break absolutely with constituted normality', and I know, having said that, I know it's becoming quite fashionable now to talk against Derrida and denigrate Derrida, and make this ridiculous argument that Derrida just relegates us into a nothing world where no one can choose anything, and anything is possible, and everything becomes in a sense the same, but this comes from people who read a small amount of Derrida as undergraduates and have never really *read* Derrida, or Heidegger, or Nietzsche, for god's sake. I mean, I should say it's not that there aren't some legitimate arguments about this, I mean in some ways Derrida is holding out the promise of a fundamental reorientation of how we make meaning itself, and in some ways he's *not*, and we can talk about that – but there *is* this sense, especially in the early writing, that it *is* possible that we can make a language and meaning system that is freer, and less oppressive, that we need so much and that would liberate us from these overrestrictions, these either/or choices and violent binaries, these *us and thems*, these *it has to*

94

be this or thats that we do get so locked into and trapped into, these overdeterminations and overcertainties and limitations that make it so hard for us as a species to think and feel and I think do make us so unhappy.

But then that's just – I – I should say I, I want to say, I want to admit that socially or familially it is a problem, in the family there is a problem, I have a problem, which is, where, you have to do things, I have to do things a normal, socialised father would have to do, right, you have to do things like take your child to the movies, the other children are socialised for this, your child is socialised for this, Issie's friends see movies, she wants to go to the movies and I don't want her to be – I mean you do have to *do* these things and eat ... popcorn, possibly, I mean I don't like it but Issie can have it if she wants it, I'll get there in line at this ... counter and buy this ridiculous bucket with cartoon figures on it, fine, that's all fine, what I *won't* do is sit through the movie itself, I'll go in and make sure she has a good seat and no one strange is near her and I tell her I'm right outside if she needs me, I'm in the foyer – I mean I just said to Issie, I said to her, Issie I don't want to go to the movie, and she said that's alright Daddy, I know you don't like movies, and, see, she's good to me, she understands, and she's *ten*. But everyone else is, my god, I told Astrid – *Issie* told Astrid, 'Mummy I went to the movies and Daddy stayed outside' – which was a huge mistake, I mean *my* mistake, god damn it – Astrid's at me, *her* mother's at me, they're all *at* me, like it was the wickedest thing in the world, this abuse – I mean she should talk about this with her own therapist, as I've said in here many times Astrid has her own troubles to do with control and anxiety, Issie was fine, I *don't* think you have to think she'll be attacked, I think it's *alright* to live like that, not to assume she'll be attacked at a 2:30 afternoon children's session at Chadstone Shopping Town; I'm *in* the foyer, I'm right there, I just need to be in the foyer, and Issie knows she can come and get me if she needs to, I'm in the foyer, so she's alright, and I'm alright, I mean I think you give, but you don't have to give *everything*. Right, I mean does that sound alright? And when the thing is finished she tells me the animals got to the land they wanted to get to, or the princess fell in love, or whatever it is, whatever the stories are, and that's fine, that's actually fine, that's quite nice, I actually don't mind that at all, I'll hear it from her, but the whole time that's happening I can sit in the foyer and read. Just *read*. And I know, alright, right, I know it's not ideal for a father to not be able to be with his daughter when she watches something, when she's having that experience, that amount of experience, I know, but we're friends *outside*. Not in the movies but *outside*. I love her. But it's not … I mean, this may be where my affective experience may be quite wrong but you have to also decide what you are going to do and be and how you are going to think, and I think our civilisation has got the amounts of this very wrong, and, again, this may be where my affect and my investments are maybe quite wrong but I think it's not a mistake to *be* strange and to, to – have my own thoughts for a while? I mean how else are we going to do anything *better*?

A NIGHT WITH
THE FELLAS

Well hello boys, hello fellas, my name is Josh White and I'm a bit nervous up here, so bear with me, I'm certainly one of the younger blokes here tonight from the look of it, but I'm the one who has to sort of start the proceedings tonight, and this night, it certainly has become a bit of a tradition, just over the last couple of years, a lot of things are changing, but this night, it's become a really special night for us, just something that we realised we really needed to do, as sort of more traditional Australian men, we sort of realised we needed to organise, in a slightly more formal way, just to get a sense of where we are, as a group, but also just for the chance to be together and so tonight all over Australia blokes will be gathering for this End of Year Night With the Fellas, blokes who grew up together, or blokes who went to school together, mates from the footy club, mates from work, it doesn't matter, so long as you get together with some mates, or in this case a couple of hundred mates!

And we're obviously going pretty good, just judging by the turnout here tonight, and it is just fantastic to see so many fellas here tonight. And I just want to give a bit of a special thanks on behalf of all of us to the local Fellas Committee, Damo, Sooms, Letty, Reefs, and all the boys, I had a bit to do with it this year, and I saw the work they do to support the night, so thank you to all the boys for all the work they've done, and we're really lucky to have all this, the hall, it's looking pretty classy I'd have to say, bit of a step up from last year, all the tables, and quite a bit of classy velvet around, so that's good, and I should just say, great work to the local Fellas Committee, for all the work they do, the tables, and the display, the pictures of the sporting legends up there, that's always good, so thanks to the local committee, thanks for doing all that, thank you to them.

OK. I'm getting through! It's all good. Now, I've got this bit of paper here, hang on, here it is, I've got some special thank yous to give out to some fellas who have made a pretty huge effort to be here tonight. A Matthew Neale is here, he's come all the way over from Marimba, where are you Matty? Thanks, mate. And a Luke Hirst is here all the way from Sweden! Might have to ask you for a bit of a report on them Swedish women, mate! Yeah, yeah. Later, later. OK. And Brodie O'Keefe and Brad Dunn have got a special thank you to give to a

Mark Werrens, where are you Mark? And I've got here that Mark, he's a local boy, now living up north, up there in Bowen, and apparently he got married *yesterday* and then hopped in his truck and drove eleven hours just to be here. And that – how is that? That is a really special effort. That just shows some of the commitment we've got going. No, absolutely, round of applause. Above and beyond, mate, above and beyond. Some would say suicidal! And I do have an extra message, Mark, from Dunns and Keefes, who say, 'Marky Boy. You have proved yourself for all time. What you have done tonight makes the Anzacs look like they weren't even trying, this is Kokoda stuff, that is crazy brave. Dear Mark all your mates wish to tell you that what you have done today is just magnificent and very, very foolhardy. And we all, your good mates, wish you the best of good luck with your missus when you get back home, we will be nowhere near you!' So a beautiful note of support there, from Mark's mates. Top work, fellas.

And so now, just in terms of the format of tonight, from here it'll be pretty much exactly the same as last year. We'll have this bit, this opening bit, and then I'll do the personal revelation, which I'm not really looking forward to! And then after that, the entrées will be served. Then we'll have the video presentation, the sports highlights of the year, the great moments in cricket, in rugby,

and AFL, and the lighthearted moments, your bloop-
ers and your classic stuff-ups, and then of course your
chance to vote on Legend of the Year, and also Disgrace
of the Year and who should go to the Doghouse. And if
any fellas don't have a vote card, that's this little card
here, please come up and see me, or Soomsy, but every
bloke should have one. And then after that, mains will
be served. Then after that, I asked Ron – and I should
have said before, a lot of you will know Ron Thwaites
over there, he's a bit of a legend himself, bit of an elder
statesman, for a couple of years now he's been our local
Fellas Committee chairman, and, anyway, I asked Ron
what happens after mains, and Ron said, 'Then we just
drink till they throw us out.' And I did think fellas would
be pretty happy with that, as a plan. And Ron obviously
continues to qualify as a legend, just by that remark.

OK, so with my bit now, this is the personal revelation, and the committee did decide this year to keep
on with this sort of more modern element of the night,
and – can all fellas hear me OK? Yeah, no, we should
probably settle down a bit, just those fellas up the back,
could fellas maybe just pop back into their seats, and
the fellas who are also in the middle, sorry fellas, yep,
OK, I'm just getting the word here from Ron, the drinks
will be served to your tables, fellas, so please stay seated
if you possibly could, the staff are doing their best, and

drinks will be served to your table. Alright. Good. Thanks fellas. Sorry fellas. It's all good. I've just got to press on a bit. So now this bit, this part, the committee did ask me to read this, this is the national committee's mission statement from last year. OK. Mission statement:

> With the challenges of new ways of being in society continuing to impact on Australian men, we are coming under increasing pressure to learn new skills, including a much greater reliance on emotion and personal revelation as an integral part of everyday life. As a result, local committees are asked to encourage all members to share their personal stories and revelations with other members in a safe and welcoming environment, to facilitate understanding and respect, and with the ultimate goal of enhancing our cohesion and position as a key leadership group within Australian society.

OK. So there you go. I'm not sure I followed every bit of that, but the committee's obviously thought it through, and it's certainly true you should always try and learn new skills, and so I'm happy to go along with that. So I am gonna do this, the personal-story element of the night, which I have been a bit nervous about, but

I did talk to a few of the boys who said they enjoyed it last year when Aaron talked about his manic depression. So I do want to say thanks to the committee for making me do this, even though I really don't want to do it!

So I was thinking of what story to tell you, something a bit personal, but I was worried it was all sort of not eventful enough, maybe, I had a pretty normal childhood, not really any sort of big bizarre events, no Darwin Award-type capers or any of that type of thing. And I'm pretty normal in my personal life, so sorry to disappoint any fellas out there who are a bit AC/DC and playing it a bit strange! Yeah, thank you, fellas. Like I say, whatever you boys do is whatever you boys do. But I did think of one thing that did stand out as sort of a funny story that happened one day when I found all these sex books in my mum's closet.

Yeah. Thank you. I'm glad that got a laugh somewhere. I'm not too sure about this story, but I wanted to tell it, I don't know, I thought, maybe it's a example of funny things that happen when you're growing up.

OK. So it's just, one day I found a sort of pretty big stack of sex books hidden in Mum's part of the closet. And what was *I* doing in there, you might ask? And that's a fair question. And I think it's just that, Dad's at work, Mum's at work, you're a bored kid, and sooner or later you're gonna do *something* that you're not supposed to do.

My mate Macca, he used to light fires when his mum and dad went out. Just little ones. And I'd go round and I'd help him. He'd do it on a sheet of metal so it wouldn't go further, and it was good, out the back of his house, we'd burn all this paper. But with me, I just loved to search the house. Just by myself, I'd go through the whole place. I've always loved like, secret passages in movies and stuff like that. So anyway one day Mum goes out and I find all these books, right down in this big bag that has all her summer shoes in it. She had so many – you know these books? – you see them, fancy lady romance type of things, but they're actually quite chunky little things, they're like 500 pages or something, with, you know, big gold writing on the cover and these pictures of some lady and some bloke on some yacht, or in some really rich place, some castle, you know. Your pretty standard lady romance sort of business. But these ones were a bit more – out there. One had a picture of a lady's arse, just that, sort of hanging there, and some guy's hand touching it. That one, that's the one I actually remember the best, that was called *Hot Lights* and it was by Torri Lee Stanzi. And I always remember I thought it was so weird that she had three names, no one in Mill Park had three names I reckon. But anyway I kept goin to get it, when Mum went out, I must of read bits of that book like, fifty times. It was about this guy Zac, and he had this big disco nightclub in New York, and he had this big rivalry with this other guy called Donnie, he's another disco owner. So it's all like, battle of the discos. And which one can be the best one in New York. And Zac, he's a pretty ruthless sort of character, and there's these two twins, Stefanie and Charmaine who are Van Meers, and they want to ruin Zac's empire. So that was all good, I quite liked all that. But then it would, you know, get right down there, and there were some things I just did not understand. The first time I ever found it, the first bit I read was this bit where the twins are plotting against Zac and so they both decide to give him a blow job. In his office. To sort of trick him or something, make him weaker, I don't know. In the book it was sort of confusing, partly because I'd have to say I only half understood what a blow job *was*. Yeah, yeah, thank you, I know now! I know *now*. I'm saying *then*. I knew it was a sex thing. But I'm like, they blow on his willy? Is that good? So I was a bit lost, and, this was what really got me, the whole point was that Zac, he was really bored of blow jobs, the book said he'd had so many, it's just nothing to him now, does nothing for him, it's over. So the twins get up on the desk and put their fingers in each other's arse and he watches that for ages and only then can he come. I was like, Jesus. It was a lot. I was pretty little. Like, I was still in primary school.

Anyway! That's that story. Whatever I did or did not understand about what was exactly going on there, it was certainly a memorable day at home. I don't know. It was all pretty random. Anyway, maybe other fellas would have a similar story from their younger years? I hope so. Hopefully it wasn't just me! Or my mum! But anyway, just thanks for listening to me and that's it, and now with huge relief I can get off this stage. Thank you fellas. Good onya fellas. Thanks for listening! Enjoy the sports presentation!

CURRY

Queens' Hotel,
Townsville,
17 April, 1930

My dear Father,

I am not certain whether you shall get this in chambers or at Ballerea, but please do write return or send a telegram, as I am not sure of how to proceed here, and I am in need of your counsel. The facts are in the main as I stated in my last to you, however some new matters have come to light, and I did go with Dudley to see the native prisoner at the watch-house to-day. He is said to be a most intelligent lad, for a half-caste, but he would not say much to me. Dudley got from the detective that the charge will be wilful murder and not manslaughter or procurement to ex. a crime:— this was before we went down to the cells. Dudley says I can be his junior and of course it goes heavy into the balance in my mind that this would be my first appearance before a Supreme Court, and would get me noticed by Lockhart, and the bar here, and Webb, and all the Phillips St fellows. And indeed we would be, as Dudley says to me, by some lights at some rather clear advantage, as the real difficulty for the Crown is that it will be deemed quite reasonable to say that the superintendent was quite insane at the time the native lad shot him down, as the superintendent, Curry, had already murdered his own children and attempted to murder the settlement doctor and his wife:—by shooting in the instance of the doctor, and in the instance of the wife by beating with a rifle butt. It will further be adduced that Curry then placed paraffin and gelignite explosives inside his own house, the general store, and the school for native girls. All this is already in brief, in spite of what everybody here says is the very peculiar difficulty of procuring admissible evidence from native persons who are generally uncivilised and whom were in nearly all cases sent to the Palm Island settlement for offences committed on the mainland such as refusal to obey administrators' orders, or refusal to work:—however notwithstanding this we <u>do</u> have the depositions as to Curry's quite precise whereabouts at the various times of the night and day, and as to his activities, and though it is true the witnesses are all natives, that is because it has now come out that as soon as Curry began his rampage, all the other white officials on the island, after some I take it rather hurried consultations, retired to the interior and hid themselves:—all of this will be given out in open court, as will I think the entirety of the history of bitter quarrelling between Curry and the other white officials on the island, and that a magistrate's inquiry last year heard most serious allegations against Curry for drunkenness, against the settlement doctor for drunkenness, and further against Curry for the flogging of a native girl so badly she could not walk, and that there were the several allegations that Curry had sought connection with young native females.

That is all on one side. On the other side is that the magisterial inquiry, though it may, judging from some letters he wrote, have contributed to the superintendent's mental disturbances, found no evidence whatsoever that the superintendent had interfered with the native women, or that any other serious misconduct had taken place, and that, on the contrary, he, Curry, was found to be a most effective officer, who had been at his post for more than 10 yrs and had attained a very high degree of efficiency in the administration of the island, getting cattle going, building of roads, &etc. I saw old Edwin Gough on the Strand, and he said to me that prior to the tragic events of the night of the 2nd the man had a very good record of service indeed. And I must underscore and have perhaps not made quite clear, that there is a great deal of ill feeling and back-biting here that any black on the island should have been permitted to bear arms, and to patrol about the streets, and then to lay at ambush, and then shoot down a white officer in plain view of the whole community.

So you see I am in a quandary. It is a question of whether I want to get further mixed up in this business, which seems to me to reflect no credit upon the white officials on the island, but also goes to points of law which I feel I may not be able to properly advise upon. Please do tell me what your opinion of these matters is. I may still take it. What I <u>would</u> do if I <u>were</u> advising is to begin by pointing out that the current imprisonment of several of the other natives who were present, in view of the fact they are merely witnesses, and are not charged with any crime, may count as a provocation, or a contempt, injurious to trial, &etc, and that this should be put to the jury, following the rule in Kepple's, and R v Copse. But Father please telegraph <u>to-day or to-morrow</u>, and tell me what your more experienced judgement of these matters is.

Yours with all my affection,

Tom

NAURU

██████ ████: There are five. Sorry. Six. Five males and one female. The female is housed in a separate unit.

██████ ███████████: They're an interesting group. I try to take an interest in them personally. We've got one PM who wants to exercise a lot, and that is a challenge. And I've tried to accommodate him, but it's hard on gravel, the camp area is gravel, and gravel is hard on the footwear, and he is wearing thongs, which are not ideal for running, frankly, even at the best of times.

██████████ ██████: There's Glooms – he's the tall one, moody prick, I don't like him. Then the little bald one with the hearing problem, he's Deafie, we call him Deafie, we did that on the first day. Then the other little one, Bowl Boy, little bowl-haircut boy, he thinks he runs the show. And the Silverdick one too, him and Bowl Boy, they both never shut up. Then – who else? – oh yeah, Captain Fitness, with the ears, and the redhead. She's The Sheila.

████ ██████████: Oh, Bowl Boy, so many stories. First day I was here, he was telling me how to be a guard. Explaining my responsibilities. And I'm just looking at him, thinking, 'Mate, if I was you, I wouldn't be telling me what to do.'

████████████ ████████: Yeah, it's sort of like a big construction yard. Or a quarry? Like, it's just gravel, with a fence around it. And then tents. And then, they live in the tents.

████ ███████████: When they first got here, they used to have a lot of meetings, and sort of give talks, to each other. You'd see the six of em out in Area 3, making all these lists and doing all these diagrams with a stick in the gravel. Havin the big meeting. Good on em.

█████████ ██████: Well, it's heat, it's humidity. It's tropical, tropical conditions. And there's a lot of mosquitoes. So yeah.

114

██ ████████: Oh, you do see the human side of them, and that does affect you. The female one, she has no kids of course, but you see the relationship she has with her nieces, you can see that's quite a strong bond. You'll see her waiting to Skype with them, and sometimes the connection goes down, IT here is pretty bad, but you'll see her there, at the OP2 shed, waiting and waiting for it to go back up. You go out of the camp and come back for your next shift, and she'll still be there, sitting on the steps, just waiting and waiting.

████████ ████████: What a lot of people here don't understand is that these PMs just want someone to listen to them. And I do try, I try to listen to them and I think they can be interesting, but what I do find is it's better to get them off the human rights side of things, which is all they want to talk about, and it really is just better to try and get them to talk about other things. And they can be quite interesting, one of the males, he seems to be quite a learned sort of person, the other day he was telling me about these religious people in the past, St Aquinas, and this man Bonhoeffer, and I thought all that was quite interesting.

██ █████: Cappy Fitness, he loved it when we took them for a swim. You can do little excursions outside, out of the camp. Take a coupla guards, go out for two hours. So we took em to this place, it's a concrete boat ramp but it's the only place on Nauru you can swim, cause the rest you go out and you get cut by the coral. And it was nice, you know, or at least, it was a lot better than the camp. It took weeks to get it approved, we went through all this palaver with the Department, I should show you the files, all the emails, but eventually after about five hundred emails and meetings with DIBP, we actually got permission to take all six of em down to the boat ramp. And Fitness, like I say, he was in there like a bullet, splashin round, splashin the others, doing these laps, he is a mad concentrated fella. But the others had a go, had a splash around, even Deafie went in. But then later, a coupla weeks later, back at the camp, the whole thing with Deafie's wrist happened and that, that was in the camp, but I think the Department just thought, you know, if him or one of the others hurts themself out of camp, that's liability trouble, big trouble, and we're not gonna start flying these people back to Australia for surgery, so that was the end of the whole swimming thing. Shame really. Every one of them went in for a bit and had a swim. And it's – it's pretty hot up in the camp. But you've probably heard about that.

████ ████: Well no one wants this. Of course. No one thinks this is an ideal situation.

████████ ████: The funniest is her and Bowl Boy. Sometimes he won't even come into the Rec Tent if she's there, it's like he hates her. Other days, he's runnin across the compound to her, askin her this, askin her that, I don't know, showing her some new bit a paper he's written all over. And they jabber jabber on.

████ ████: There was, yes, an incident with a PM where the PM slipped on a gravel incline approaching the steps to the toilet demountable and the PM fell and he did sustain an injury to his wrist, but the IHMS people were able to come and assist him and give him that assistance to get him up and about again.

██ ████: I don't know. Just a lot of doubts. Two of them are fairly old, and they need a lot of medicines, medications, and I just think, physically, they shouldn't be here. It's not healthy. And one of the other more younger ones, he has some sort of heart condition. But I mean, all of them have some sort of health problem now even if it's just skin, or something else, like a skin or eye infection, or some other thing like that. Or lung. The tall old one, Glooms, he just coughs all day.

████████ █████: Yeah yeah, I saw it. Deafie, he just went right off the top of those shitty slippery pine stairs. We ran round and saw him face down in the mud with one arm under him, and we got him up and he's wailin in that funny weird voice of his. Still. A broken wrist though. It would hurt.

████████ ████████: Well, that is actually not correct, your assertion is incorrect. Mould and moisture issues have now been successfully addressed in both the male and female PM marquee accommodation.

████████ ████████: They try to be cheerful. The silver one does. And the fitness one, who's always running, doing his jogging, he gives you the thumbs-up. But I also think they feel ashamed at times and that their lives are a failure. They sometimes communicate that to you. And I try to help when I can. I say to them, don't let this process get you down. You're not worthless. You got to keep that sense of yourself, even here, that's so important. You're still a person.

████ ██████████: I reckon Deafie's gone down a bit. He's had a injury, he's had the fall, and I don't think he's come back too good. I look after him, you know, when it's meals, I give him a tap, cause he can't hear sometimes, and he's in pain, I think, he's just not with it, so I give him a tap or a hand signal, just to go, go on PM, take your cup up. Otherwise he misses out.

████████████████████████████: Any PM may submit a form C2 at any time requesting they be provided with new footwear or any other article of clothing if the articles are damaged or broken however security personnel may carry out searches of PM bedding and personal effects at any time to ensure shoes are not being hidden and the request C2 is a valid request.

████████████ ██████: But you do get the weirdest examples of like, humanity here. Like, Bowl Boy, the others, the other PMs, they all hate him, but then they'll help him sometimes. Even Glooms. Cause you know, Bowl Boy, he talks and talks but then some days he won't come out of the tent, he can't do it, but I hear Glooms in there, sayin to Bowls, come on, you got to get out of this tent. Just really trying to say to him, come on, come on. It'll be alright.

████████ █████████: They all have shoes now. Shoes or thongs. I can tell you that very confidently, and some have more than one pair.

███ ██████████: I reckon it sort of breaks them in little ways. Like, even after a couple of weeks they lose their ability to do anything. Cause everything they have to do a request form for. Like even if they want tooth-paste, they have to fill out the form. And no toothpaste comes so they fill out another request. And then after a while they've filled out all their requests and they just sit there.

█████████████ ██████: I don't really follow it too much, to be honest with you, mate. PMs. They're all the same.

PM████ became agitated in the Computer Room OP2 when told by CSO█████ and myself that his time was up, PM████ asked if he could have more time as PM████████ had not appeared for his rostered session, PM████ said PM████████ was in IHMS, I informed PM████ I could not confirm if PM████████ was in IHMS and advised PM████ he would be processed back into PMRPC1, PM████ expressed this was "unfair," I requested PM████ exit computer room, upon which PM████ became more agitated, I advised PM████ again that he would be processed back into PMRPC1, I requested PM████ stand, PM████ brought his head down rapidly on computer keyboard, PM████ did this several times causing bruising/abrasion to PM████'s face.

Action taken:

1. PM████ taken to IHMS 17:05

2. Informed Team Leader O9 17:40

3. Informed Operations Manager 17:45

Signed:

CSO ████████████

CSO ████

CSO █████████████ / witness

CSO ████████ / witness

O9/W2/C/D

██████████ ███████████: Oh, I think they're disappointed sometimes. Obviously they're disappointed. They didn't foresee this outcome, and of course they question it. They question whether all of this is necessary. But then there are other times when they have expressed to me the view that, yes, we can understand why we are here, and that although it is an outcome we would not have wished, we do understand it, we understand why it is necessary.

LEADER

PRESS CONFERENCE MR MICHAEL RAY

GREAT COURT PARLIAMENT HOUSE CANBERRA
--TRANSCRIPT--
E&OE

MR RAY: OK. OK. Well, we had a big night last night. A big, big night. A big night for me, for us, for the party, and there's a lot to do today, some important meetings, so I'll get this part over pretty quickly. I'll just make an opening statement, and then I look forward to your questions.

First, let me just repeat what I said to a very, very happy crowd of New Australia supporters at the Maroupa RSL Club last night: Australia, we're coming back. We are coming back. And you know, I represented my state and I represented my country, with great pride, great pride, and I'd have to say even that wasn't as good as this.

I feel very personally humble, with this result. And I think people saw me as a player, yeah, OK, a rugby person, but also as a person, as a father, as someone who loves Australia. So I want to thank people, the Australian people, and this is a vindication, this is a vindication for us and I feel that. And now, and we can't be sure of the final numbers yet, but it does look like we will have at least forty-eight seats in the House of Representatives, forty-eight seats in the House of Representatives, it's big, it's a big change, and we may go as high as forty-nine, maybe even fifty, depending on a couple of close calls, and we'll wait and see what the good people in Lalor and Port Adelaide decide, but good on them anyway for giving us some of the biggest swings in the country, swings to New Australia of more than twenty per cent. But we saw plenty of that last night, plenty of big swings all across the country, and plenty of old politicians in a panic. So ladies and gentlemen, this is a beautiful day for Australia. We're coming back. But what I want to say to Australian people is this: I know that over the last couple of months it just feels like we're all just victims of weather now. There is no doubt that we have had some very, very nasty surprises in the environment and in our weather and unprecedented hardship and real tragedy for people, for the Australian people. The relocations have hit people very, very hard, and so many have lost their homes or even a loved one. Australians will not forget and will not forgive the failure, the systemic failure of the NHA and the Home Relocation Program. I have seen the pain that people have endured and continue to bear. But to all those people in Fremantle, in Brisbane, in Newcastle, in Melbourne, who still suffer injuries, or have lost everything, and are just waiting and waiting for some assistance, for some help, and help never comes, I say to you we're going to do all that, we're going to compensate people, those packages will be done, those packages will be put in place, help will be given, we're going to get those relocations done, we're going to protect our living standards and the Australian way of life. We're going to have a proper decent life in this country. And we do have a very serious situation coming towards us longer term now with food and with food security and with food allocation. But here's what I want to say to ordinary Australians. I say this to the Australian people. Stick with us. Stick with us. It's all very new, all this, what's happened, last night, but last night was huge and we are getting very close to a situation where we can run things, we would really be in there, and we could really do some things for Australia. This is a crusade and a viral movement to save Australia. And we've got a lot of energy up in these last few weeks and months but people need to now not go away. So if you possibly can, in the next couple of days, come on down, because we're really going to step it right up, the rallies, and if you're not with us yet, just come on down, come on down and see what we are with your own eyes, come on down to our events and the family days, come on down and hear our speakers, the boys are travelling right round Australia, you'll see the boys out there in the New Australia colours, they're disciplined boys, they're going to be out there, in the community, doing the good things, playing sport, getting food to the kids and the old people. We're going to keep the pressure right on. We can do this. We can do this. Because there's so much we still want to do to help people, help us help each other. And you know, I said, I said last night, I talked about when I was a kid, my family, we lived out in the suburbs, up in the Northern Beaches there, up there in Brookvale, up there in Narrabeen, me and my brothers, we'd ride our bikes in the street. Just Aussie kids. Playing in the street together. And we would go to the beach, you know, and then go back home and have a barbie tea out on the decking – Dad, Mum, us kids, all together. We weren't hurting anybody, we weren't doing anything wrong. We were just good people. Australian people. And I'm saying: we still are those people. We still are Australian people. So if you care about that, about a good Australian life, about safety, and water, and food, join us, and I reckon we might just save this country.

OK. OK. And with that I'm very happy to answer your questions.

JOURNALIST: It's being reported this morning that New Australia party members who were on their way to a victory celebration in Woolpara last night attacked and severely injured a seventeen-year-old boy. The boy, Adnan Al-Ebadi, is now in a critical condition in Bankstown Hospital. What is your reaction to this, given that this is the third incident this month where New Australia members have been charged in connection with a brawl or serious assault?

MR RAY: Amazing. That is amazing. You amaze me, Tracey. Even for you, that is quite an effort. OK. Give me a second here. Give me a moment. The biggest single change in Australian politics, in maybe fifty years, maybe ever, happened last night. OK? A third party now has as many seats in the lower house, the people's house, as the Liberals, or Labor, the same two old geriatric parties we've had shuffling along forever. And last night: bang. Something big. Something new. I don't know if you noticed any of that, Tracey. Maybe you were doing your hair.

--JOURNALISTS INTERJECTING--

MR RAY: Were you doing the hair, Tracey? I suppose you got somebody else to do that for you. Somebody else does that for you?

--JOURNALISTS INTERJECTING--

MR RAY: Sorry, Trace. Don't like it? Don't like the big Ray?

--JOURNALISTS INTERJECTING--

MR RAY: I now see young Tracey over there looking a bit po-faced. A bit lemon-lipped, as my mother would say. Don't you worry, the Chinese will keep paying you. Your employers, the big corporate media, they'll keep taking that Chinese money.

--JOURNALISTS INTERJECTING--

MR RAY: Yeah, look, OK, I know this will be a very new concept for you to get your head around, Tracey, and I wouldn't want to upset yourself, but I'm not actually here to talk to you. I know. I know. You are very important. And no doubt three seconds after this is over you'll be in front of a camera somewhere telling everyone what your Chinese corporate media employers want all this to mean. The Chinese corporate media employers. But if it's OK, I'll just talk, me. I'll just talk to ordinary Australians, without the meaning getting wrapped up in a lot of Yuan.

--JOURNALISTS INTERJECTING--

MR RAY: Yeah I don't need any remarks from you, Tony, you've got as much Yuan up you as she has. I think you might of dropped one, Tony. There's a Yuan on the floor there. You go get it, mate. You do that and I'll talk to the Australians.

--JOURNALISTS INTERJECTING--

JOURNALIST: Answer the question.

MR RAY: I just think it's sad. I actually just think it's sad. This huge thing happens, something millions of Australians helped make happen, but silly media people like Tracey Halliday – and I say the name, I hold you as an example, and you know, I might make a joke, no one in the media can take a joke, but I sometimes make a joke, the sort of joke that normal people make every day –

--JOURNALISTS INTERJECTING--

MR RAY: Excuse me, may I please speak? May I please be allowed to speak? I'm speaking for Australian people and Australian people are losing their homes. OK? People are losing their homes and you just sit there. I was with the families in Newcastle. I was there after they lost everything. I'm talking about compensation. I'm talking about fairness, and that transition to the new economy. I mean, it really is an amazing system you've got going, luxury for you and then all this concern, this compassion for the minorities. I see these princesses of the media, princes of the media, questioning me, all so concerned and so compassionate for the minorities. It's a great game, isn't it, raking in the cash and then being the moral arbiters. The big moral arbiters. But then of course we know it's always for these tiny little minorities, that's the game, and here you are again, with your inquiries about this one minority person, one minority person, and an incident we don't even know about, on a day when the actual huge majority of Australian people have had their say about this fundamental issue to them, this absolute issue, which is whether millions of people are going to have a home. It really is unbelievable you keep going, and I've said this, you know, it's a great tragedy that you've done this and we actually lost ourselves there for a while, it's very hard to get back from this, this absolute weakness, and we actually lost an entire generation to these little tiny identity battles, fighting over these tiny percentages of the population, every tiny little minority, and the constant fetishisation of that. And we got stuck in there, in the minority mindset, as a society and a culture, stuck in there, putting all our energy into these sideshows, into all these little campaigns, we had thirty years of that, trying to make us try and understand transgender six-year-olds, transgender six-year-olds or something equally horrible, and in the end it was just self, self, self-obsession, people playing with nothing but themselves. I tell you, New Australia, we are against the selfie culture. We don't have time for that anymore. We got to get out of all that, we'll die if we keep fussing around with all that little luxury thinking. We've got stuff to do.

JOURNALIST: You have stated —

MR RAY: And by the way, the gays love me. OK. The good ones do. Everyone knows some good gay people, and the good gay people know that things are getting very serious now, and that all that old identity crap was getting us nowhere. And they're happy to tone down some of the more excessive stuff, the party-times stuff, and get into line. Because they actually see what they could lose, they have respect for property and the good life in Australia. They want to be safe like everybody else, and they understand I'm not coming for them. Same with the Indians. The good Indian here, he does his work. He understands very well the last thing he needs is a bunch of the worst people here, the scum of the world, the mass refugee scum, these refugee convoys, and mass marchers, the real bottom-of-the-barrel people, they're the people he just got away from. That's why I get Indians, Muslims, coming up to me all the time, and saying, 'For God's sake, keep doing what you're doing, keep that scum out.' They want to stay in their homes, they hate the scum worse than I do. So don't you worry, we've got room for plenty of kinds of good Australians in our Australian family, and New Australia's getting in plenty of people the chitter-chatter media said we'd never get.

So there you go. That's how people actually think. That's how I won, too. OK. Can I get a proper question? Simon?

JOURNALIST: Michael, you've always said that you would refuse under any circumstances to form a coalition government with either Labor or the Liberals. My question is: given the unprecedented results of last night, are you now reconsidering your position, and under what circumstances, if any, would you be open to negotiations?

MR RAY: Well, that's a very interesting question, Simon. And you know, Simon, I can't think of a time before when I would have ever found that question so particularly interesting. It always bored me in the past, all this little speculation about coalition, Simon, but I do suddenly find a new interest, I do. And the short answer is that I will talk to the Liberal Party and I will talk to the Labor Party. But just to make things really clear, just to make it all nice and clear and crystal to both the Prime Minister and the Leader of the Opposition, I say to the Prime Minister and to the Leader of the Opposition: I will talk to you. I will. But neither of you would want to make any mistake. About who'd be in charge. About what the people just said they want. I say that to the Governor-General too. In case he was thinking of waving his little vice-regal wand and trying to make governments with no majority. He can just stay up there, in his mansion, and be quiet.

JOURNALIST: Have you spoken to the Governor-General?

MR RAY: No. I'm sending him more of a public message.

JOURNALIST: Your former deputy, Greg Olsen, put out a statement last night saying that he believes the party's newfound success will only lead to, quote, 'More getting into bed with big business, and selling out New Australia to its secret corporate donors.' When will you make public a full list of all corporate donors to the New Australia Party?

MR RAY: Oh, little Greggy. Don't you worry about Greg. He's OK. We had to let him go. We tried and tried with him, but Greg is – look, he was a good mate. And there would be a lot of people out there who have had a good mate who started to have problems in his life and psychological problems. In these very, very difficult times. What I would say to Greg is, mate, you just keep on trying to get your life together. As for what he is very sadly saying, anyone who thinks I'm just a plaything of big business just has to look at the twenty-five per cent penalty tax I'd put on the bad multinationals. That's what I've got in store for big companies who don't do the right thing by Australia. And they will feel it. They will feel it. But let me tell you this as well: there's no way we're going to get out of the very, very serious problems we've got with home relocation and the Home Relocation Program and getting people away from some of these coastlines, and getting to a real energy guarantee, an energy guarantee, that protects communities and loans and jobs and income and people's livelihood, you're not going to get to any of that without the help of some big companies – if they can play by the rules. I say there'll be plenty of room for the good companies under a New Australia government. Every good Australian will have a place. We'll have the good companies working with the government and the army to get great results for everyone. It's not going to be a problem. But look, with all this, I'd just have to say, it's also – it's just poor old Greggy being Greg. I don't know where he is now with all these conspiracy theories. But it is sad, to me, more personally, I'd have to say, because he was there, you know, back in the day, in my professional playing career he was there as my manager and as a bloke who could see my potential and the analysis and the vision I was making and the things I really wanted to do for Australia beyond rugby. And he got me to Stevie and Haddo and the boys at Save Australia dot com and the whole social media presence we were able to build, and those were great days, great days, you know, when we started to get a sense of just the sheer amount of feeling out there, that anger, and how big this really was, and what people really needed, how much they just needed some ideas and some hope and some leadership. But it all got a bit complex for Greg, and he's got his issues and he doesn't cope too well with the pressure. Anyway. We really do wish him all the best, with his statements.

I don't suppose I could get a policy question? I mean, careful though. I wouldn't want any of you to think too hard.

JOURNALIST: On water, you've made a number of big, vague statements —

MR RAY: Yeah, OK, before you try that one, just for the record – I had to ask you, didn't I? I had to ask you to stop doing the little gotcha stuff and ask me a serious question. OK. And what is the real situation? The reality is, in water, in food production, in everything, is that we need to apply the technologies we have, using some coal, some coal-fired production, for a limited time, so you're using coal resources in that highly effective way, for a limited time, so you're getting to that double pipeline of jobs, the double pipeline, protecting the old jobs in the old economy, getting smarter and more efficient, while of course continuing with the emergency works and the emergency operations, while all the time you're bringing the new jobs, those new economy jobs in, but we will decide, we will decide, we are going to make the decisions about our lives, based on the needs of actual people and actual communities. And this is it. This is what I'm about, this is why the Australian people have chosen to listen to me and to hear me and follow me, because I'm the only one who's figured out the next question. Because the next logical question is, the big question, the only question now is: what are we going to do with us? Not with a lot of so-called refugees, but with the people who are here and should be here. What are we all going to do? Are we just going to go our separate ways? Run around crying? Everyone just trying to save themselves? Or are we going to make something proper, and stronger, and a team? And you know, in the campaign, I talked about a bloke, Damien Nadanic, I met a bloke called Damien Nadanic up there in Tyett, up there in New South Wales, he's got a family, he's lost his home to these terrible storms. And he just asked me, 'Why? Why are these things happening?' And I said, you know, some people think Damien doesn't matter. And I suppose that's up to them, their conscience. I just think we might try something a bit different. We might try and help Damien. And all the men and women and the families in his community. And the rush to a general decarbonisation doesn't have to be the holy writ, the holy mantra. There's plenty of smart things we can do. No one has to lose the value of their home. These horrific losses of the value of their home. And we are learning what to do during any extended heat event, but we can do better and we can be much more aggressive on fire, I'm not just talking about detection and mapping, but the new technologies that intervene directly into the convection stream, the super cannons, and the chemical-retarding agents, delivering those pay-loads by plane, and if we can just throw off the shackles this government has put on us, there's an army of jobs out there, an army of jobs, and we can actually get going with those very effective new technologies, not to fix everything, not as a panacea, but simply to buy the time, we should be utilising every strong new technology we can to buy the time we need to make the bigger economic adjustments we're going to have to make. And that, that is just common sense at this point. We need to strengthen everything we're doing, as a people, and make that effort to really lift our performance at every level so that we're able to cope with these fires and this heat and the drought and with food supply and with the transition to a new economy, and we'll be able to get those problems done.

JOURNALIST: The Leader of the Greens —

MR RAY: No, no, I've said it before, I say it again, I will keep saying it: Greens are not a part of politics. Greens are not a political party. Greens are death to Australia. They are the climate criminals. They have lied to you. They cannot not lie. It is in their deepest core. I put it to her, you all heard me, I put it to the Leader of the Greens that she had stated that in ten years there will be a thirty per cent loss, a thirty loss of arable land in New South Wales. And we know in the secret documents, the secret Green documents, we know it said five per cent. Well, which is it? Which is it? Which is it? Five or thirty? That's people's lives. That's people's livelihood. And she says, 'Oh, that's just an adjustment to the figures. That's just the decadal smoothing.' The decadal smoothing. The decadal smoothing. That's clever isn't it. They're so clever, these people. And she is for reparations. She is for reparations no matter how much she now pathetically attempts to deny it. She is for us paying poor countries money, because we're the dirty polluters. But it's worse that that, it's even sicker and more dangerous. The Green says it's our fault that their countries are ruined. I'll say that again, because incredible and pathetic and sick as it sounds, the Green actually really does believe this: it's our fault that their countries are ruined. I said before about Aussie families, little Aussie kids riding their bikes in the street. What does the Green say? Those families were evil. Those Aussie kids were evil. Evil polluters. Evil Australians. And we owe the brown villagers reparations. That's what the Green brain makes. That's what they think is practical politics. We did better, we made something, but in the sick, twisted Green mentality that means you should be punished. She'd have the people of Newcastle out there living on an oval forever, in tents, living in the dirt, living in these unbelievable conditions, because she cares more about people who don't even live here. But we know what she is. We know these people.

They're elites. They can't help us. They've been so-called educated till they've got no basic common sense. They can't see normal things. She'd just have another seminar and another panel and another agenda and another summit and then maybe some more panels. Because that's what we really need isn't it? More panels. But I say to you everything I do is based in that crucial understanding of what has happened to real people, real Australians, and its effect on people's lives. And you know, you really just have to ask yourself whether we should really just start to put our faith in the sort of people who can actually do something, like the ones in the army, and the Freo Volunteers, and the Fire Force. And haven't they been doing a wonderful job in these very, very difficult times?

OK. Last question, before I go over to the PM's office, have a little look around in there. Last question? Oh, Trace. There you still are. You little terrier you. You well-paid shihtzu. It's all in fun, Trace. I hope you can take a bit of a joke, it's not like any of this matters or anything. It's not like the future of the whole country is at stake, I can easily stay and hear more from you. OK. OK. What was your important question?

JOURNALIST: A follow-up question on the boy who was assaulted last night. I was informed just a few minutes ago that the boy has died. He died about an hour ago, after undergoing an unsuccessful operation to stop internal bleeding. Bankstown Hospital won't give out a cause of death, that of course will be for the coroner to determine, but a spokesperson at the Bankstown did say that the boy, Adnan Al-Ebadi, has been properly identified as being only sixteen years of age, and that he suffered more than thirty knife wounds to the head, arms, chest and abdomen. And that his parents, Aisha and Ibrahim, were with him at the hospital when he died. And I just wondered, Mr Ray, whether you had any further comment to make.

MR RAY: Yeah. Yeah, Tracey. I suppose I do. I do have a comment to give to you. Let me think for a moment. Just so I can get it, get it right for you, Tracey.

It's funny isn't it? People wouldn't think I get tired. But I do. I get unbearably tired. I get unbearably tired of you, Tracey, and all the people like you. The people who will never, ever understand. Who will never see what I see, in Australia, out in the suburbs, out in the bush. Who will never understand what it really takes to make this, this nation, that we want, this nation. This nation. And that the blood of the West will survive and will live in the South. And you know, I was a professional athlete. I was a professional athlete. I could have stayed at home, very happily. Very happily. And my kids – OK.

OK. You know what? Here we go, here's the truth you can't take. Get this, Trace, here's what's coming soon, and you and your kind have no idea. I know what you think I am. I've had that all my life. But I can see things. I can see some things. And what I see is: we're coming up to a very big time. Soon. That's just history, that's just the way it works. In history, sometimes, not often, but sometimes, you get a really big new time and big big changes. Very basic changes. And after that we can have the good times again. And just to be real clear: I'm not asking you to help. You media, the elites, university people, all you people who think you're so clever, but have never understood what the world really is, I do have a special promise for you and all the others like you. You're on the way down. We're on the way up. I can just feel it. It's all going one way.

OK. OK. So I reckon that'll be enough for this morning. Thank you. And for the future, well, I really do wish you people the very best of luck.

WATER GIRL TY TUCKY

WATER GIRL FURY

Water Girl SHOCK Storms Out of Interview, What Made WG Storm Out of Interview With Ex Ty Tucky

Water Girl TOTALLY LOSES IT in Interview with Ex Ty Tucky, What Revelation Completely Shocked Water Girl WATCH NOW

If you've been following the saga of Ty's efforts to reconnect with Water Girl after their one-year hook-up and divorce, you'll know how high the stakes are when they FINALLY meet ... in The Angel Spa. WATCH NOW

REPLAY
SHOW MORE
COMMENTS

chrissen

Haha so funny. I love you water girl!

amieG

Hehe loved Water Girl

jdop

Cool

beezer

dude is just arm muscles and a tiny dick as well

annajesky

so beautiful!!

isla

love love love RESPECT X

jarvis

haha at 3:40 Ty is like whaaa....................??

Dore

she's hot

popk

ty as interviewer hes really good

EricaR

lol

suss ali

TY: YEH THIS IS SERIOUS!!!!! IM TAKING MY
SUNGLASSES OFF!!!!!!!!

atman

she is so hot

shessoB

WG IS A STUPID TEEN BLONDE ! TY PRETENDS
HE STILL LOVES HER ASKS DO U STILL HAVE
FEELING FOR ME THEN BASCILY CALLS HER
A SLUT THEN SHES SOOO OFENDED THEN
ITS ALL FAKE WHAT A FAKE DRAMA SHOW IF
SOMEONE DUMP YOU WOULD YOU TRY GET
BACK WITH HER IN A SPA ! IN PUBLIC.......HELL
NOOOOO...........THATS THE REAL THING!!!!!!
THIS SHOW IS SO MESSED UP!!!!!!!!!...
Read more

deserise

lol i knew it was a prank the whole time as if they
wouldnt warn her before he was going to say that lol
there just doing this for publicity

ringu

SHE IS THE GOLDEN WATER QUEEN

tom styli

I thought it was real

pauls

god when she stands up at 3:28

lolakat

A WOMAN ANGER!!!!!!!!!!!!!!!!!!!!!!!!!!!!!!!!!

ion70

I cant believe we have a water crisis and people are watching this

mel

wow they acted really good

kusja

wow tys acting was so believable

lizzilD

did he THROW the sunglasses?! where ARE They??

REPLY

5 replies

> **olivia k**
> on the side. at 2:12
>
> **fawcet**
> i want them
>
> **joanna voll**
> I would make them a SHRINE with LOVE!!
>
> **mattih**
> in WG ass
>
> **mattih**
> her twat

ashelaqueen
im mad i thought it was real and she was really upset!!!

julia conrad
see in the audience girl in red shes like whaaaaaatever

creebin king
TY IS #1 ACTOR FOR REAL

harperh

OMG that spa

liam beeps

NO she WAS really angry but her manager told him to say it was a joke

flatdg

she so pretty

katyaB

I thought this was real

dechanted

Ty is such a good actor

shannne

its nice they crak up at the end there friends and its not real that shes upset with him

widy

so cute love

ashe little

TY LOOKED SOOOO UPSET HE SHOULD WIN ACTING AWARDS LOL HE IS WASTED DOING VIDEOS

148

shootsthebadguy

lol

declan p

shes amazing

sweg

i want that spa!!!!!!!!!!

Dr Spaceman Troll

I like when ty says i respect your privacy thats good
coming from the ultimate media slut king

supergeekking

I THOUGHT IT WAS REAL

bunicorn

Ty needs it in da ass

itshayden

she obviously didnt want to talk about it so she got up
and left. stop making a big deal about it.

anna carrott

IT WAS A PRANK

deni

I like the big guys hair

alonzo rad

that red chick in the audience is not into it

starblaze

wg looked really upset she is soooo CUTE!!!!!!!!!

daneg

this is freakin hilarious

smann

shes so hot

dsg

I find this really creepy

sususan

Did Ty Tucky go out with water girl?!?

puccafromstjames

That looked soo real

crshed

very good ty now you are a actor yay yay

cat love

oh I was literally going to complain about ty for wg then i saw it was all fake!!!!!

ADY

I was shock to see this. it is sad

pattyd

is this real??

spulr

no pipewater soon and people watch this crap

carl

dumb dumb dumb

kerii

she was actually really angry but the producers told her to be nice and get back in

connorhall

Ty is king! Like this comment if u agree!

connorhall

Like my comment if u agree!

trevor
Interesting reaction from the girl.

neale
people need to realise the problem with this kind
of content is that (a) for years even before so much
population faced up to all year restrictions or places
that are losing pipewater the majority of population
was turning increasingly to anything to get their minds
off their problems and turning to stars who are people
like Ty Tucky as well as the more negative people
and effects and we know that long term this has very
negative effects but its mostly just the problem of this
has existed for years with negativity growing and b)
people need to think of real H20 solutions now not
get lost in pointless hating we know this has been a
problem for years so lets concentrate on solutions eg
reclaim greywater eg porta desalination eg zero days
not blaming people like Ty Tucky for everything after
all hes is just a product of the system were all under
and the necessity is to work to change the H20 system
and find real...

Read more

REPLY

6 replies

natti

yo lick my balls

stahlstahl

lick Tys balls is what i want

princit

oo you total cuck sheeps

moss

its just a joke weezer cant u take one

billybobdeluxe

Ty would smash yr ass

lena77

its FAKE did u even watch it to the end?!????

amymacancroe

ty is so sexy if peopel spoke to me like that i woyld say yessss

BJ

hahahahahahahahahahahahahaaaaaa

jesky

she didnt even look at him the whole interview

punk nugget

ass ass ass ass ass likit

tallulah

see tys face at 3:21 he totally knows shes going to crak it

jamesjames

shes so hot

danepower

I WANT THAT SPA!!!!!!

vnbi

i feel bad for the man the lady is not fair to him

mrblor

this is such waterporn

emmabertovic

it freaked me out I thought it was real

gocats

I think people should not give it away its prank before
people watch it

jenny

At first I was like "what a bitch" but then i figured
out it was a joke and i was haha and she seems a good
person really nice

lensentry

see her not even looking at him in the interview so rude

BAMMBBALICIOUSSSSS

water girl is a waste of space

joncarr

this is so stupid dumb dumb dumb dumb

saraht

people comment negatively when they havent seen the
video people are stopping only half way thru see the
whole thing before u judge

dente pido

damn shes hot

_punter

wg should totally get ty back and do a new prank lol

ash

I know this is a prank but i think ty has real feelings for her in the middle part i would have too

BONE2

yes you made me look at this crap

zzparktheshman

the amount of people who dont watch to the end but still give their comment.....

grimmy

How Ty is not bigger star is beyond me he is very talented

jade

I thought it was real!!!

cupo

Its not really a prank Ty has a good point at the end which is we have to love each other and care especially since we have so little water now and have to look after each other and try and be together and share h20 and other resources

sian9
i cant understand this

pantha
wow ty did such a good job if it was me i would have cryed or freaked myself out

alexbelle
I thought he was really upset best actor goes to Ty

warn
hes such a good actor!!!

nicatt
she hot hot hot what a ride

xndrtron
he still loves her how could you not love ....
THAT BODY!!!!!!!!!

janusjustice
I cant be the only one who thought this was real....

smashdit

ITS A PRANK JUST WATCH IT TO THE END

tzrealwater

This was not an act. this was real. Ty Tucky was ordered to do this. Then laugh it off as a joke. Visit my page www.tzrealwater.com follow me at @tzr6water

BFNAARK

ty got the rags

vgliet

so funny!!!!!! Ty is the best actor!!!!

theBrody

i thought it was real but wait till the end its fake

lucyp

its not real u see wgs face you can tell she's waiting for ty to ask her if shes already in love again and hes smirking

erici

I feel bad for him because people always ask him about wg and she moved on pretty fast

daniela

I love it when he goes "watergirl u are something beautiful from my past, the past is beautiful but it must remain in the past etc we all had to learn that" what a wanker

summer20

I love Ty's "SERIOUS" face

peaceluvnow

so funny!!!!

melindas

Sorry to bring this up but you know this isnt real??

adda

TY TUCKY "FEELINGS"!!!! OMG

romy

shes so cute adorable

hawkq

people this is really sad if u hate wg so much why are u even watching this clip!!!

pslattery

Ty has a point at the end which is theyre here to talk about water saving not personal life

dee

didnt know this was a prank wow!!

nickman

DO NOT MESS WITH THE TY!!!!!!!!!

saveourplanet

ty is my king

jhead

THERE ABSOLUTE CRAP

ozanat66

water free deposits SECRET locations @ozanat

bz

haha great how did she do that without laughing!!

kaminiyfrog

oooh! I'm taking my SUNGLASSES OFF!!! THIS IS SERIOUS!!!!!

kyliem

I feel bad for wg but then its a prank haha i get it now

genna

im so glad that wasnt real!!

sensationalle

I thought that was real!

tgatz

I cant hear it!!! Why is she upset!!!?!!

MISSY

From: genevieveteale@amail.com.au

To: georgiat@highfern.com.au

Date: Thurs, 11 Jan at 10:14 AM

Subject: Hello Darling

Dear Georgie,

It feels like ages since I've written to 'catch up' and see how you are up there at Highfern. And of course give you the gossip from here!

How are things with you? I'm fine and David's pretty well. Of course it's very hot down here with these being the absolutely worst weeks forty six yesterday we've just shut all the front part of the house up completely now and don't use the sitting room or the library or any of the east facing rooms, they were becoming quite intolerable. David took our old barometer with the temperature thing into the sitting room this morning at 10 and it said already 35 degrees at 10! He thinks its all so interesting of course he'd take the barometer into every room all day if I let him but I said that's enough barometer thank you very much. The big thing now is everyone ripping up their carpets they don't want them anymore because of all the insects and the dust you should see it in Stanthorpe St out the front it is odd you see huge rolls of carpet.

But we're very happy doing our 'camping' in the kitchen where there are the tiles. And it is so much worse now for so many people I always think, old Roger in that awful little unit in Hawthorn lying down in the bath half the day because he's so terrified of getting heatstroke. I saw Dianne Sutcliffe the other day at the food drop and she's having a really dreadful time with Hamish. I imagine the disabled have a very difficult time now quadriplegics or paraplegics with no electricity for them, you hear such dreadful stories. Di has to keep going at that rotten little hand generator for an hour just so Hamish can go up and down the hall a bit in his chair.

But I do have a 'happy' story which I think you might enjoy. Libby has certainly become quite the 'Queen of Tasmania'. You would have heard of her big time success but I got an email from Ross Trengenning the other day and he was really down there at Christmas and saw it all and he says it really is this fabulous place, who'd of thought it would be Libby Hayes but she's held on and it really is one of the last privately owned vineyards in Australia. And Ross can you imagine he had to be at some dreadful food drop out of Launceston for Libby's people to come and get him at 5am!! But you know Ross, he'd go to the Sahara desert if he thought he could get one last glass of cab merlot. Can't you just see him waiting with his panama on and bow tie and his tongue hanging out of his head though bless him, he did get himself right into the high security estate or whatever it is and saw the whole thing this fabulous green valley. She apparently gets a tonne of water. The army gives her extra credits would you believe and Ross went to a lunch where they were all there the army, the ennies, the reg police, they're all around Libby's table for a lovely tasting. And of course everyone else pays a fortune. Dear God the prices she gets!! Ross said some madman in Sydney paid her $15 000 for a bottle of pinot gris. It just shows where we're up to I think and I think certainly the government has some questions to answer for.

But anyway enough about old Libbs! What I wanted to write to you about darling and I'm sorry because you must get a lot of these enquiries, but I was wondering whether there was any space coming up at Highfern.

The situation here in Malvern is really not good and I
just say to you very frankly (this is just to you) that I was
hoping that David was going to be a bit more proactive
and show a bit of activism in terms of our situation here,
as there's a real chance we should now be finding some
other accommodation and that's why I have written to
you. I thought it would be more the thing just to send
you a quick enquiry but don't take any trouble, just let
me know when you can.

my love to Brian,
love from David too of course
Gen

From: genevieveteale@amail.com.au
To: georgiat@highfern.com.au
Date: Fri, 19 Jan at 8:38 AM
Subject: Highfern

Dear George,

Hello I'm just following up, I don't know if you got an
old email I sent you about a week ago full of news about
Libby Hayes of all people. And some news about old Ross
Trengenning!

I was also interested in asking if there were some vacancies at Highfern in the next six months or so or even next year. David and I are pretty 'keen' to get out of Melbourne soon.

Your friend,
Gen

From: genevieveteale@amail.com.au
To: georgiat@highfern.com.au
Date: Mon, 22 Jan at 2:50 PM
Subject: Re: Hello Darling

Hello darling and thank you for your wonderful note. It was so wonderful to hear from you. Yes, we are all in good health, Mum and Dad are really very good. It's a new thing for our generation I suppose to take our parents 'back in' but the terrible heat situation we're all in now of course makes it absolutely necessary and we're very lucky of course to have a bit more room here though I think I told you last time we can't use most of the front of the house, those high French bow windows which I loved now they're just awful giant magnifying glasses. So we cower in the kitchen! or the laundry would you believe. Dad had a bit of an 'incident' the other day when he got so fed up I think with sitting in the back of the house (which is still pretty hot but I say to him please stay there Dad because the bathroom or laundry are really the best for him, he is 83) but bless him he took it upon himself to go for a 'walk' outside if you please at 1 in the afternoon it was probably 50 and there was Dad tottering down Stanthorpe St in his Huntsman's wool jacket!! Meanwhile there I am at 1:30 saying to David I can't find Dad and then the mad search in all the front rooms nearly suffocating and then I was so sick with worry out in the streets out in that oven with my umbrella sweating like a pig I don't mind telling you, then Michael Elliott rang and said I've got him. Apparently Dad got as far as the corner of Wattletree Rd and Glenferrie and then just stood there in the middle of the intersection. Thank God there's really no traffic anymore. We were just really very lucky Michael saw him, Michael still goes to his private practice on some days the energy police take him and he said to the ennie boy who was driving stop, I know that man. I don't know if you know Michael he was really very high up at the Royal Melbourne quite a big surgeon there before they moved everything up your way he was head of Orthepedics. And Michael had a good look at Dad and said there were no physical injuries thank God and Dad's been resting here under my orders! But it does make it more urgent for me to do something about finding other accommodation so thank you again for sending me all the basic information and those prices are quite acceptable and look like something we can do and I can say with confidence please do send us the application forms as soon as possible, the whole family here is just very excited to start the application process as soon as possible.

Thanks again,
I'll write with more news soon!
Gen

From: genevieveteale@amail.com.au

To: georgiat@highfern.com.au

Date: Wed, 24 Jan at 9:02 AM

Subject: Application process

Hello Georgia,

Thank you for the application forms and your extra email questions.

I want to be absolutely upfront about Dad, and I can reassure you that he is fine, that story was more just a personal story but the point of that in the end is that he was examined by a very eminent senior medical doctor and found to be absolutely fine. And of course I'm happy to put you in touch with Associate professor Michael Elliott who is former Head of Othopaedic surgery at the Royal Melbourne Hospital and he will be very happy to give you a full report on Dad's situation which is one of very good physical health and no significant mental health concerns other than the heat confusion that of course is now a very common occurrence among our elderly senior citizens.

As I say, I am very happy in further correspondence to furnish any further medical documents and details, and I've got the whole family working on their parts of the application pulling financial documents from here there and everywhere so I think you'll find I really think we're in pretty good shape and suitable for Highfern.

Best regards,
Genevieve Teale

From: genevieveteale@amail.com.au

To: georgiat@highfern.com.au

Date: Mon, 5 Feb at 12:52 AM

Subject: Application for Residence at Highfern Private Reserve

Attached: **davidcrieffteale.pdf genevievemayteale.pdf jameswilliamlees.pdf gretamargaretlees.pdf charlottemaykeppell.pdf jeremykentkeppell.pdf noelkentkeppell.pdf anneelizabethkeppell.pdf tobykentkeppell.pdf zaramadelinekeppell.pdf missyteale.pdf**

Hi George,

Here it all is, in record time. The property statements are at the end. You'll see some of the discretionary trust things are mine and David's together, except where some of the funds already go directly to the trust for the little ones, in which case those assets appear on their forms. Jeremy and Charlotte's forms are a little confusing in so far as they include some of Jeremy's parents trust, the status of which is unclear. But I've included the letter from DT Advisory which should shed some light. I checked some of this with the very helpful Fiona in your office and she said it should be fine but let me know if any problems and we can resubmit at the double.

Please don't hesitate to contact me if there is anything else that you require. And thank you so much for the opportunity to do this.

Fingers crossed!
Gen

From: genevieveteale@amail.com.au
To: georgiat@highfern.com.au
Date: Fri, 16 Feb at 9:14 AM
Subject: Hello

Dear George,

Just wondering if there was any news with regards to our application.

Charlotte and Jeremy moved in 'officially' with us yesterday with the little ones, which was lovely.

Better weather here, dust not so bad in all streets.

Hope you're well. Love to Brian.
Gen

From: genevieveteale@amail.com.au

To: georgiat@highfern.com.au

Date: Tues, 20 Feb at 11:22 PM

Subject: A check

Hello Georgia,

Just checking to see if you had received our application forms, there should be ten, and a special one for Missy. And if everything was alright, and if there was any more information I can provide.

Don't hesitate to contact me if there is any more detail I can provide. My son-in-law, Mr Jeremy Keppell I think may also have sent you an email to introduce himself, and to give you his best wishes.

Yours sincerely,

Gen

From: genevieveteale@amail.com.au

To: georgiat@highfern.com.au

Date: Mon, 26 Feb at 11:27 AM

Subject: hello

Dearest George,

Just checking in to say hi

The heat is really getting us down here, there's not much to say I wish I had some news for you. Roger Seddon sent David a thing about new technologies and decarbon bots and David is very excited about that.

I understand from Fiona you really do get it sounds like hundreds of enquiries every day but if you possibly can in the next few weeks, do please let us know if there is any news at all about Highfern.

Gen

From: genevieveteale@amail.com.au

To: georgiat@highfern.com.au

Date: Mon, 12 Mar at 4:55 PM

Subject:

George please send some response I emailed application to you five weeks ago still no response.

Gen

From: genevieveteale@amail.com.au

To: georgiat@highfern.com.au

Date: Wed, 21 Mar at 4:16 PM

Subject:

Georgia

I'm sorry to write to you like this but I am worried and upset because it's been nearly two months now I have received no acknowledgement of my family's application for permanent residence at the Highfern Private Reserve. I am looking at other reserves of course, Georgia, but you are my preferred option because of the security and position Highfern is able to offer our family. I have made enquiries about the Meridian II in Sorrento and Agora at Mount Martha but I feel both these locations are too vulnerable due to their proximity to sea and strong winds and storm surges that our coastlines increasingly suffer and the recent flooding of the Portsea area and difficulty of evacuating residents of course is very much on my mind. But Highfern's location in central Victoria in Macedon valley and your reputation for very strong security are persuasive to me, as well the situation here is becoming quite uncertain with the energy police becoming quite intrusive often stopping people in the streets even if they are residents of that street they have been EXTREMELY rude to me this morning when walking a very short distance with my father I tell you this incident as a key incident of our times now, eps making us stop and surrounding us they all looked about seventeen they find it all so amusing that dad's got on an old t-shirt of Davids with 'Action man' on it calling Dad 'action man', I said right up to them his name is Mr Lees thank you very much and one boy taking a GUN out I said don't you be ridiculous. Then they have to have their little moment of triumph making me empty out all my bag which is only an old calico bag with a towel for Dad and water from our water drop LEGAL I showed it had our sticker on. And all this with poor Dad standing there. They are just bullies and I told them so. You just hear continuously how the ep are rude to citizens and reports very disturbing of ep taking things from homes of residents without permission and now at the end of all this day I find out our very old friend John Petherill has been in a very serious incident he has been expelled from his residence in Albert Park he and his wife who I know well we don't know where they are we have NO NEWS of them.

Please send me news soon,

For our old friendship,

Love,

Gen

From: genevieveteale@amail.com.au

To: georgiat@highfern.com.au

Date: Wed, 21 Mar at 5:24 PM

Subject:

i think its completely unreasonable that you and your people give absolutely no acknowledgment of applications which are sent in good faith and do require considerable work and time from the family concerned and it is very poor business practice and extremely treatment of people

From: genevieveteale@amail.com.au
To: georgiat@highfern.com.au
Date: Wed, 21 Mar at 6:41 PM
Subject:

Dearest Georgia,

This is to apologise for emails I sent you I sent you two
emails earlier today one about an hour ago and another
one about half an hour before that and I do apologise,
if you see them, please do disregard both of them, I've
been a bit upset today because we had some trouble with
the energy police they were mean to dad and I found
out a very, very old friend of mine Susan Petherill, her
husband John has got them into some very bad trouble I
don't know what's going to happen Im very worried for
her and angry at HIM its HIS fault John I never liked
him the fool always big noting himself he still has a private car for Gods sake but they got an evac from their
bit of Albert Park, which they knew was coming it's the
south they're practically on the waterfront and they got
approval for Sienna at Bonnie Doon which I know you
would know is a really very good reserve. But then its a
month and HE still won't go I said to her you've got to go
and she says John doesn't want to yet, then they get their

red evac so finally he gets in that bloody car and he says he wants to take Morgan he's their King Charles Spaniel which was NOT the plan Morgan was supposed to go to Alistair's (their son) but John thinks he can just change an evac order the ennies wont stop him because he's John Petherill well of course they stopped him of course they stopped a private car they stopped them at Warrandyte, took one look at the back seat and there under a tartan rug is Morgan. And John and Sue had to come back to Melbourne to a PUBLIC RESERVE. Sue was texting me but now no more from her I texted Alistair and he doesn't know. I'm sorry to have sent wrong emails to you I am very sorry I was just upset I think because I think Sue could get sick in a Public that idiot commissioner says now he HAS to say after all the nonsense there IS cholera in them they say you don't get one bit of water without queuing for God knows how long and those crowds in the heat I'm not good in big crowds I get very anxious and then with Dad it would be quite impossible. But I apologise for those earlier emails I understand that many people must be putting lots of pressure on you and I have to be brave. David doesn't help me.

With an apology,
Gen

From: genevieveteale@amail.com.au
To: georgiat@highfern.com.au
Cc: fionad@highfern.com.au
Date: Fri, 23 Mar at 4:45 PM
Subject: missy

Dear George or Fiona,

Thinking about our application I was wondering
whether the presence of our dog Missy was a problem
and whether I should have done more to explain why she
was included. I understood from the application process
and the documentation you sent that pets were allowed
provided each pet had a separate form and provided that
the family could prove that of course it could meet the
significant extra costs and it was my understanding from
conversations with Fiona that certainly the inclusion of
a family pet was not a potential problem for the success
of the overall family application. But I wonder now if at
this time when the general situation does seem so much
more serious, whether it would be better to ask you if the
inclusion of Missy in our application is creating problems
and if Highfern has a quota of small dogs it can take in
any given admission period.

She is my dog more than anyone else's and I was the one who did want her to come with us and it would be hard for me to withdraw her application but I do see it was wrong to put her in, but when David was at Corrs group and the kids were gone she has really been my friend for a lot of years, I have tried hard to keep her through all these times I've worried about her so much in this heat she is very adaptable and very good and I do think the maintenance is adjustable I find, I keep her topcoat very short in these conditions and even though there is less meat of course, not even chuck or bones, she will have sweet potato or the pumpkin now and the soya every other day which is not easy for an active little dog (she is a West Highland Terrier). But it all has been hard and I know things are really changing now. Let me think it over, I do see it but please let me think and I'll write again soon.

yours,
Gen

From: genevieveteale@amail.com.au

To: georgiat@highfern.com.au

Date: Mon, 26 Mar at 5:40 PM

Subject:

Please send me something whenever you can re our application.

Gen

From: genevieveteale@amail.com.au

To: georgiat@highfern.com.au

Date: Tues, 27 Mar at 6:03 AM

Subject:

Darling if you get a minute please send me some news.

Yours,

Gen

From: genevieveteale@amail.com.au

To: georgiat@highfern.com.au

Cc: fionad@highfern.com.au

Date: Wed, 4 Apr at 1:34 AM

Subject: A Change

Dear Georgia,

I write to formally withdraw the application of Missy Teale for permanent residence at the Highfern Private Reserve. The other applicants contained in the original application are still valid, but Missy is not to be considered.

Please acknowledge receipt of this change to our application.

Yours truly,

Genevieve Teale

From: genevieveteale@amail.com.au

To: georgiat@highfern.com.au

Date: Fri, 6 Apr at 6:14 AM

Subject:

Darling

if you get a minute please send me any news.

Gen

From: genevieveteale@amail.com.au

To: georgiat@highfern.com.au; fionad@highfern.com.au

Date: Tues, 10 Apr at 7:22 AM

Subject: Application

To Georgia or Fiona,

This is an enquiry regarding our application Family name Teale.

Our registration code was H464553, do send news if you have any, available. We would appreciate any response. If there are any questions you would need answered please do not hesitate to contact me.

Genevieve Teale

From: genevieveteale@amail.com.au

To: georgiat@highfern.com.au

Date: Thurs, 12 Apr at 11:33 PM

Subject: from Gen teale

Things are very bad here, as you know. David and my family and I are asking you to help us at this very desperate time.

Gen

From: genevieveteale@amail.com.au

To: georgiat@highfern.com.au

Date: Fri, 13 Apr at 12:55 PM

Subject:

My family and our children please ask you to send any news.

From: genevieveteale@amail.com.au

To: georgiat@highfern.com.au

Date: Mon, 16 Apr at 4:55 PM

Subject:

Please send me something

From: genevieveteale@amail.com.au

To: georgiat@highfern.com.au

Cc: fionad@highfern.com.au

Date: Tues, 1 May at 2:54 PM

Subject: Well.

Darling the first thing I want to say is just thank you, thank you, thank you. On behalf of myself and David and the whole family we are just ecstatic here I did of course know that you would come through for me, my old friend, and I thank you and Brian and Fee and everyone in your office for doing such a wonderful wonderful job up there, it must be a very difficult job indeed and I just want to thank you for your work at this very difficult time when so much is uncertain in our society. You provide a secure place for families who desperately need it in this really terrible time we are all going through and I thank you. You are my superstars. I can tell you the whole Teale and Keppell family is just so happy and relieved. Our youngest grandson Toby is very excited and is making a Highfern 'hat' he is going to wear! And mum and dad are absolutely thrilled of course. We will see you at the main gate on the 23rd.

And I want to thank you really personally too, George, the 'pressure' really got to me in those last weeks but as you pointed out to me I understand you receive hundreds of emails every week and I should have had more faith in our application which was very strong and in us as a good family and in your good and very thorough process of vetting and selection. As you say and as Fiona did say to me, these things take time, the proper checks have to be made, and I can understand you have to be careful in these really very uncertain times. David says to me the financial system is not what it was and you just can't know any more who really has capital they can keep calling on. And I did send you a couple of messages where I really should have 'zipped it' a few times there! But I will say thank you again and I will say I am absolutely thrilled that Missy is able to come too, to take my special little girl with me really has been 'the icing on the cake'.

With much love and gratitude from the <u>whole family</u>, your
Genevieve

BUNKER

i found this so im going to use it it feels uuummm to be writting with a pen i just have to write a little every day

my name is mikayla i live in 5cc im writting this so ppl will know about us !!!! we r here it used to be a carpark now its for pple we have to do clening and disenfecting what you get relly sick of is all concret and remebering nice things from the surface. at nite pple cogh and i wake up. when its blackout then its scary we just sit there. i cant think of anything else goodbye untill tomorow

soo today we got soup it was ok it had some vegies in it and i got 1 ricie

hi today we did disenfecting i was with a new family milns and a old lady maree

hi today we did dis and cleaning

today we did cleaning

today we dint do anything its hard writting u can see why ppl didt do it

hi today more new pple came they are from sydney

today rencos said were not alowed to hang cloths on any walls coz it makes more lice come all the pple arked up lice will come anyway and were are we supposed to put our cloths they dont fit on the bed with us there

hi today more ppl came they went to 4

today we did cleaning and dis

today more ppl came rencos made us move our mats im in 5tt

today more ppl came everyones getting freaked out

today team leader adam came and gave a speech soooo long about renco how the companny is helping us and rules i fell aslep!

hi today we got soup and 2 stickys

today i did cleaning from all 6jj - pp

today we wipped and did disinfecting

today in the sydney ppl i saw this chic i know van !!! she was in our res when we were there. i told her my mum and dad died and she said hers died too. were going to meet tomorow

today i saw van she said our bunk is better than cogra there relly overcrowded

today i did cleaning i got 1 pac 1 sticky

i did clening

i feel bad were really hungry

i hung out with van

today the rumar is were all going to go melb or to tas

im so hungry. i did cleaning then i just layed in bed

i cleaned on 8 were rencos are they didnt let us see it relly but its cool and not many ppl

i did cleaning i got 1 pac 1 soy

im itchy bites on my legs fkg bad

today more pple came they went to 4

today i went to 7 to get extras but there were so many there u coulnt breath. i tried to go the side but i coulnt i waited ages i got 1 soya 2 stickys

today the rumar is that well get only 3 pacs a week from now on

more ppl came now i am in 5gg theres so many pple here now

i had a dream where i was with dad and mum and we were at lara st when i woke up i felt so fkd

mmm i have not many cloths left

today after cleaning we got potatos

today i feel better we got tatteys again

today there was a talk abut lifta6000 in our bay by this guy peter it was ok ppl do it its abt god and personal Story having positive better feelings

my team was suposed to go to 8 but then they said no cleaning today

today in one knee it hurts. i went to cleaning but

today we had 1 soup and 1 sticky

today evriones going about the girl who was at 6ff and she lyed down and she died

today we had a speech from tl adam

today ppl were freaking out bc adam said we have to tigtten our belts

today the family next to me had a big fight bc dad took the kids pacs and ate them

a lot of ppl are doing pettitions and sitting down they wont work

i am scared coz ppl r loosing there shit in here

i dont know where van is her mats not there and ppl said shes on 4 but i cant find her today there was no soup we just sat there

today i want 2 say if any 1 finds this later this is what it was like and so ppl should never do this

today no soup i feel sick all day

im so tired i cant think of anyting

today they said now we have to go to 7 to get pacs or stickys its to far

today my head hurts i feel bad

today no soup ppl we just lie there

raf in my bay went to hospital

theres droppers in the stairwell. 2 ppl did it they were married

i had a dream we were dyeing mum dad and me. i have so many fkd up dreams in here now

today i did cleaning

i feel relly sick

today i read some of the lifta book. i did a personality test thats in it

today i feel relly weak it hurts in my toes in my toenails. what is that? i piss from the shit soup theres nothing in it. i dont want to be golum. im scared. i will do wiping 5 days if adam lets me

i hope that when it happens to me im not freaking out and im ready

u will survive u will go beyond the surface u fall u rise

lifta is peace. lifta is calm. lifta is the power to rise

i did cleaning today. we got 2 stickys

humanity has 6000 years. then we reach litmus. this suffering now but we wait in udus bad earth as long as possible then we go to elos. so this suffering now then humanity lifts so we suffer to show the plan 4 luv.

i know i can b stronger. i know i can become strong. find my elos self. lifta is the luv u know

l.i.f.t.a. love. for all creatures. i intelligence. f. fidility. t. tenacity the will. altitude. to lift. lift.

today i didnt go to cleaning im too sick

today i went to cleaning but i fell down so they brught
me back here

i try to get up from the bed but i feel sick

ppl never can help us i feel sick

sick today

i felt better i got up

i slept all today

u feel better. u be better by tomorow. u get up.

i felt better i got up

i feel better

Sean O'Beirne is a bookseller and critic. He grew up in Melbourne's outer suburbs, and studied arts, law and acting. This is his first book.